The Killing Ground

Charles R. Pike

CHELSEA HOUSE
New York, London
1980

Copyright © 1980 by Chelsea House Publishers, a division of
Chelsea House Educational Communications, Inc.
All rights reserved
First published in Great Britain in 1977 by Granada Publishing Limited
Printed and bound in the United States of America
LC: 80-70090
ISBN: 0-87754-239-2

Chelsea House Publishers
Harold Steinberg, Chairman & Publisher
Andrew E. Norman, President
Susan Lusk, Vice President

A Division of Chelsea House Educational Communications, Inc.
133 Christopher Street, New York 10014

CHAPTER ONE

The first bullet took the man through his left arm. It ploughed a bloody hole through the soft flesh between elbow and shoulder, ripping muscle to ragged tatters before blasting between two ribs, puncturing the lower edge of his left lung, and lodging itself against his spine.

The second hit him while he was opening his mouth to scream. Because he was falling sideways off his horse, it missed his heart and hit his thigh instead. It ruptured the heavy muscles controlling the knee, so that his leg flipped upwards, lifting high out of the stirrup to turn him sideways over the panicked horse. He slid across the saddle, dead fingers dragging the reins back to turn the animal's head, haul it round in a circle. The third bullet clipped a chunk of hair-freckled bone from his skull, and blood gouted thickly into his eyes. It streamed down from the wound, clouding his failing vision, smearing his face with a sticky, scarlet coating.

He tasted it on his lips as he tried to scream, but when he opened his mouth, only blood came out, clogging the words. And he died.

Up on the ridge, the man who had fired the three shots smiled and shifted the aim of his rifle. The telescopic sight was a rare thing to find in America – even more rare in the Indian Nations – but he was never without it. Now, with infinite care, he centred the cross-hairs on the panting horse, squeezed the trigger. The animal bucked once as the high-calibre bullet punched through its skull, and collapsed onto its dead rider. The man on the ridge nodded slowly, satisfied with his handiwork, and walked back to his own horse.

He walked the animal down off the ridge to a position behind, and to one side of, the two bodies. He tethered the beast to a scrub oak and reached into the saddlebags. Hunkering down, he began to chew on a piece of a dried-out cheese, watching the buzzards drift down from the clear sky.

The ugly birds wheeled in lazy circles, checking the ground before they were certain it was clear. Then they began to spiral groundwards, uttering raucous cries as they zeroed in on the unexpected feast. The man stayed quiet and still beneath the shade of the oaks: he was waiting for another kind of visitor.

His wait was short. Circling buzzards meant death, and death meant mostly people in the Indian Nations. So, sooner or later, someone came to take a look. The man had picked the place and the time: the one he expected was not long in coming. He heard the sound of hooves long before he caught sight of the rider, and climbed to his feet to place one hand over his horse's muzzle, holding it silent. From the shadow of the trees he watched the rider haul his animal to a stop and jump from the saddle. The newcomer turned the body over, gasping when he saw the ravaged face. Then he dragged it up from the ground, humping it over his own pony, and rode away.

The man in the trees waited a while, finishing the last of his cheese, then mounted and moved out after the corpse-carrying rider.

He followed the man down the draw, cut across into a dried-out river bed, then up onto the tree-lined slope that wound up to a high meadow. He stayed in amongst the trees, never getting close enough for the man ahead to hear the slight noises his horse made, but never far enough back to lose him. They rode on that way for an hour or more, lifting up through the mountain meadows, through the tall pine thickets, to a small shack built into the downslope of a fallen rock-face.

The man carrying the body halted there and slipped from his saddle. Carefully, as though the corpse could still feel, he lifted it down as a man carries a sleeping child, and took it inside.

The other man smiled and rode his horse in closer to the tiny cabin, keeping just out of sight of the grubby windows.

A jay shrieked in the branches above him as he tethered his horse, and he glanced up, one hand shifting instinctively to the gun holstered on his left hip. It was a Smith & Wesson .44 Russian, the rubberized butt as black as the clothes he wore, and smoothed by much handling. He slid the gun from the holster and flipped the knock-down cylinder open. Unused cartridges jumped from the chambers as the automatic ejection system threw them clear. The man caught four of them before they hit the grass. He slid the brass and copper tubes back into the gun, then bent down to retrieve the others. Systematically, he blew on each one to clear it of impediments before dropping it into the empty chambers of the Smith & Wesson. Then he holstered the gun and dragged his belt around so that the holster rested against his right side. He reached down to tie the thigh strings around his leg, then stood up, flexing his right hand.

From inside the cabin there came a low sobbing.

The man hitched the tails of his black frock-coat back, dragging the right side of the garment over the butt of his gun so that the rearward projection of the holster held the cloth clear of the grip, and stepped out from amongst the trees. For a tall, well-muscled man, he moved with a surprising lightness of step. His passage, as he crossed the mountain grass fronting the cabin, was silent as a stalking cat's. It matched the expression in his red eyes.

He reached the door of the cabin and paused, listening. All he could hear was the snuffling of the man inside, and the sound of furniture being shifted around. He smiled again. And kicked the door open.

Inside, the cabin was dark, the brightest point the paleness of the crying man's shirt. He looked up as sunlight flooded in through the opened door, and gasped.

'Who the hell are you?'

The man in the black suit said nothing for a moment, just stared around the shack. The other man carried no gun and the closest visible weapon was a Henry carbine hung on nails above the fireplace.

7

'You Amos Wade?' His voice was quiet, northern accented.

'Yeah.' The man called Wade sounded nervous. 'Who are you?'

'Klein,' said the man in black. 'Saul Klein.'

He stepped away from the door, into the cabin, and Wade saw for the first time that he was an albino. His skin was corpse pale, his hair a wispy silver shroud around the dead face in which the only points of light were the gleaming red eyes. They studied Wade as an undertaker might study a new-found customer.

'You shot Jethro.' Wade's tone made it a statement rather than a question.

'Got paid to,' said Klein quietly. 'You too. Seven hundred dollars you're worth. I had a helluva job findin' you. Been scouting the hills for the past two weeks without spottin' this place. Then I saw Jethro herding stolen cows and figgered he'd either lead me to you, or you'd come to him. Worked, I guess.'

His tone was conversational, disinterested. It sounded almost as though he was discussing some academic problem.

'Why?' Wade's voice was high-pitched, frightened.

Klein shrugged. 'Never asked. Colby hired me to kill you, is all I know. Seven hundred dollars says I don't want to know.'

'Jesus Christ!' Wade gasped. 'Don't you care?'

'No.' The albino shook his head. 'Why should I? I got paid. That's all that counts.'

Amos Wade had a fair idea why Nathan Colby had hired a gunman to hunt him down and kill him. He had been lifting Colby stock, aided by Jethro, for the past year. Seven hundred dollars still sounded a jumped-up price though; and he didn't like the idea of dying. Klein's eyes, however, didn't look to be giving him much alternative. He chose to make a try for life, and sidled towards the fireplace, still talking.

'How about I cut you in? With Jethro gone, I'll need a partner. It's a profitable business, an' this could be a nice little spread.'

8

Klein smiled again. 'No. The only spread you're gonna get is under the ground. The only one I want is in Salt Lake City.'

'Salt Lake City?' Wade kept easing his feet sideways, towards the fireplace. 'You a Mormon?'

Klein grinned without speaking.

'You like wimmen?' Wade was pushing now, hoping to distract the albino. 'I hear them Mormons take as many wimmen as they want.'

'Some do,' said Klein evenly.

'How come a Mormon's packin' guns fer others?' Wade gabbled. 'Thought they was all religious.'

'Some are,' said Klein.

'Long way from Salt Lake.' Wade was almost up to the fireplace. 'You come a long way from home.'

Klein smiled, watching the man's hand inch up to the Henry. He let Wade shift his weight onto both feet, tensing for the spring that would grab the carbine into his hands. He enjoyed playing with his targets like this: it added a little excitement to a boring job.

Wade moved fast – faster than Klein had expected – lurching up to drag the Henry clear of its hooks, and drop down to the dirt floor in one smooth, swift movement. But Klein was faster still. His hand closed around the butt of the Smith & Wesson, dragging the big handgun up and out of the holster. His thumb yanked the hammer back as the barrel cleared leather, and his first finger squeezed down on the trigger as the muzzle lined on Wade's face.

The rustler was slamming the action of the Henry back into place as Klein's shot hit. The carbine fell from his hands and his head flipped back under the impact of the .44 calibre slug. A gaping red hole appeared in his forehead, midway between his eyes, and a sudden fountain of blood sizzled over the burning wood. Klein chuckled and shot him again, in the chest. The body twitched, jerking under the impact. Then it went still.

Klein was still chuckling as he kicked burning wood around

9

the cabin, spilling kerosene from the lanterns to add to the blaze.

He was whistling as he rode away from the funeral pyre.

CHAPTER TWO

The man from Salt Lake City tugged a sheet of neatly folded paper from his vest and began to study the words inked on the page. Frowning in the dim light, he tilted his chair back and reached up to adjust the control tap of the gas-lamp set into the wall over his head. Someone hissed irritably as the lamp jetted a whistling spurt of gas that ignited and blazed in the artificial twilight, but he ignored the sound. Then, from the next booth, a face appeared around the screen, mumbling something about the disturbance as a hand, gloved in white silk, motioned at the offending brilliance.

The man glanced briefly upwards, taking care not to look directly at the light because that would have blinded his vision, then at the face. He said nothing: he had no need to, because his expression said more than any words. The man beyond the partition caught the look, saw the cold, dead glance that summed him up and dismissed him; and swallowed hard, wondering what to do next. His companion, who had not seen the look, grumbled softly, urging him to assert himself. Bolstered, or perhaps embarrassed, by the female support of his male dominance, the man twisted once more around the velveteen screen. This time he risked speaking.

'Sir.' His voice carried the soft accent of a Missouri gentleman. 'Your light ... It's somewhat distracting.'

The man from Salt Lake City glanced up again.

'You want to come around and turn it off?'

Miles Danvers was used to commanding plantation workers, even enjoyed bullying the junior cadets in the military academy, but he suddenly realized that he had no desire at all to step around to the adjoining booth to turn down the offending lantern. He swallowed hard for the second time, ignoring Miss Annabelle Lee, and shook his head.

'Good,' said the tall, blond man, turning back to the paper, 'then we don't have a quarrel.'

Miles Danvers shook his head, settling back in his chair with an expression that was part fear, part awkwardness on his handsome face. Beside him Annabelle Lee stared in out-raged surprise. She had been looking forward to this perform-ance of the Rossini opera. Mostly because the best-looking young bachelor this side of the river had asked her to accom-pany him; the performance of the opera, *William Tell*, was a pleasant, but secondary, consideration. None the less, Anna-belle was annoyed by the intrusive light from the neighbour-ing booth; and even more annoyed by Miles's nervous retreat. She decided to take matters into her own hands, and rose from her plush-backed seat with a haughty look of dismissal on her pretty face. She pushed aside her escort's arresting hand, oblivious to his gasped warning, and thrust her blond curls around the partition.

Then, like Miles, she gasped and drew back, choking on her complaints.

The man in the next booth had that kind of effect on people. It had amused him for years, proved useful more than once, so that now he ignored it, concentrating on the handwritten note.

His hair was naturally fair, bleached even whiter by the Utah sun to a spider-silk brightness that matched the pallor of his face. His skin was pale as a corpse's flesh, and drawn as tight over his angular bones. The pale yellow glow of the gas-light produced a waxen look that outlined his mouth and eyes with an eerie, black-limned accentuation rendered yet more macabre by the silver hair. He was dressed all in black, as though to emphasize the whiteness of his skin, to throw grave-pale face and white-ridged hands into stark relief against the undertaker tone of his clothes. And the red eyes that stared at Annabelle Lee looked capable of sucking the soul from a body and chewing it up.

His name was Saul Klein, his profession killing. He was in

St. Louis to collect five thousand dollars. And so far it looked to be an easy assignment.

He was fresh in from the Indian Nations where he had been paid a modest seven hundred dollars to kill a man called Amos Wade. What the dead man had done, why anyone should want him killed, stirred neither conscience nor interest: Klein had agreed the price and fulfilled his obligation. As he meant to fulfil this one.

Ignoring the tenor batting notes at the ceiling from the stage below, he began to read the note.

It was an old habit of Klein's, to study his assignments either in total privacy or in public places. Either way, he went unobserved: in private there was no one to see him; in public, no one got farther than his eyes. He leaned back in the chair, settling the black-butted Smith & Wesson Russian smoothly against his left hip, and read the hand-printed note. It was inked on expensive paper, the characters penned with a flourish that belied the importance – and the price – of the man described. Briefly, it described a man of short stature, well-muscled and given to wearing a grey suit of English cut, topped by a derby hat. His eyes were brown, his hair black; scar tissue crossed his nose, and his front teeth were broken. He might have been any one of the hundreds flooding into St. Louis, except for the extra identifying factor: in St. Louis, the chances were that he would be accompanied by a blind boy.

The name of Saul Klein's target was Jubal Cade. The man willing to commission his death was called Ben Agnew.

Klein settled his left hand on the butt of the S&W, and read the note through again. It had taken a month to reach him, coming overland from Fort Smith to McAllister's Station up on the Windy Ridge, and he had expended one more month getting to St. Louis to meet Ben Agnew. He didn't like the man, but the colour of his money was persuasive, and it sounded like an easy hit.

He had watched the target for two days, following him from the cheap rooming house to the plush grounds of the

Lenz Clinic. Back into the city, bored by the routine of aural sightseeing that the man followed with the fair-haired boy, ending each day at the clinic, and back again to the rooming house. After that Cade had gone to play poker in one of the smaller saloons: Klein guessed that he didn't have too much money, despite wins of around nine hundred dollars.

Saul Klein was satisfied that he knew his man: he liked to know his victim before he killed him.

Still grinning, he folded the paper and lifted his opera glasses. He dimmed the gas-light and shuffled his chair to the edge of his solitary booth, focusing the binoculars on the well of the auditorium. The man was sitting seven rows back from the stage, about halfway along the bank of seats. Klein chuckled as he thought how much the target must have spent on two seats in so prime a position at the St. Louis Opera. Then, as he swung his glasses to take in the boy, he realized that Cade must have bought the tickets to please his blind companion. The child was obviously enjoying the performance far more than his friend.

Andy Prescott was. The long months in the Lenz Clinic had both bored and tutored him, so that now he was delighted to get free of the place and enjoy some of the things drilled into him by the relentless Herr Professor Lenz.

'Jubal,' he said softly, sensing his companion's stilled fidginess, 'they say that music sooths the savage breast.'

'They also say,' whispered Jubal Cade, 'that empty pots make the most noise.'

Andy accepted the admonition even before the dowager seated behind them shushed her irritable request for silence. It was a thing Jubal had noticed about the boy ever since he was blinded: * an uncanny knack of sensing the temper of the people around him. The orphan's father had had a penchant for aphorisms that got on most people's nerves – Jubal's not excluded – and his son had picked it up, though in his case it was forgivable due to his blindness and the true grit he displayed in coming to terms with his affliction.

* See: Jubal Cade – *The Killing Trail.*

So Jubal simply smiled, and settled back to listen to the music.

And above him, Saul Klein contemplated his death.

The gunman couldn't make up his mind whether he should kill the small, grey-suited man straight away or leave it for later. On balance, he chose the latter course. The S&W Russian was an excellent gun, but he wasn't sure it could reach that far effectively; and gunplay now would arouse too much interest anyway. Saul Klein preferred to remain as anonymous as possible. So he decided to study Jubal Cade for one more day, then kill him in some convenient place. After all, Agnew's money was good for a long stay in St. Louis.

He lowered the opera glasses and eased his chair back. It had been a long time since he had heard any kind of decent singing. Not since Chicago, in fact, when he had been hired to kill a senator getting too big for somebody's boots. That, he recalled, had been a pleasant assignment: no more than three days on the job, then a straight holiday. Much like this one.

Klein eased back, enjoying the opera along with his victim.

Had anyone asked his opinion Jubal would have admitted to boredom. He had never learned to enjoy the opera, and even though his murdered wife, Mary, had tried hard to instil in him her own delight in the formalized music, he lacked the necessary enthusiasm. This visit to the Opera House was planned mainly as a treat for Andy. Since taking the orphaned youngster into his care, Jubal had seen relatively little of the boy. His visits to St. Louis were infrequent and marred by the knowledge that Ben Agnew still planned to kill him. Or, more precisely, pay to have him killed: the man held Jubal responsible for the accidental death of his wife*. That vendetta still burned fierce in Agnew's mind and, even though the businessman had given his word that Andy Prescott would not be drawn into it, Jubal was wary of some hired gun hitting the boy by accident. Thus, his visits were usually confined to the clinic itself.

This time, however, Andy had shown a new interest in

* See: Jubal Cade – *Doublecross*.

music. Professor Lenz was eager to develop his pupils' remaining senses as compensation for his lack of sight, and a music appreciation course was part of Andy's training. Aided by an enthusiastic professor, Andy had succeeded in talking Jubal into buying tickets.

'It's good, ain't it?' Andy whispered.

'Isn't,' corrected Jubal automatically. Then grinned, adding: 'Yes, I guess it is.'

He settled back in the chair, listening idly to the rising crescendo of sound, wishing he was playing poker instead.

High above, Saul Klein slid back his chair and left the box. He had seen all he wanted for now and as the opera was scheduled to remain in St. Louis for another week, he could always come back. After killing Cade.

The gunman returned to his hotel. He locked the door of his room, leaving the key half-turned in the lock, and poured a generous measure of whiskey. He shucked off his frock-coat and set a square of black cloth on the table. From a saddlebag he drew a revolver that matched the weapon on his hip, checked the load and placed the gun to the right of the cloth. Then he opened a small pouch of tools and began to clean the S&W. Working with precise movements he stripped the gun down, wiping each part delicately with a lightly oiled rag, drawing a cleaning string through the barrel, and checking the cartridges before reassembling the machinery and thumbing shells back into five of the cylinders.

Across the room stood a dark oak wardrobe, its doors covered by a six foot spread of mirror. Klein stood up, facing the glass, and began to draw the S&W. He practised for fifteen minutes drawing off his left hip; then he tugged the holster around and spent fifteen minutes drawing from the right. When he was satisfied, he began to massage his hands before washing in liniment. Finally, after almost an hour, he cleared away the tools and began to sip the whiskey.

The glass was halfway down when a knock on the door brought him from his seat. The S&W was cocked and aimed before he was fully upright and he stepped silently over to the side of the door. He stood to the right of the frame, reaching out to grasp the key. He turned it slowly and eased back along the wall.

'Who is it?'

'Got a message from Mr. Agnew.' The voice was husky, negroid. 'Said to hand it personal to Mr. Klein.'

'Door's open,' Klein called, flattening against the wall.

The messenger was as black as Klein was white, and the nervous darting of his eyes showed that he didn't enjoy having a gun pointed at his belly. He took a pace into the room, thrusting a sealed envelope at the gunman the way a man pokes a stick at a diamondback.

'Wait,' grunted Klein, holstering the revolver as he tore the message open.

He read the note and smiled. On him it looked bad.

'Tell Agnew I'll be out directly.'

'Yessir. Rightaway, sir.' The messenger grinned his relief, hurrying away before Klein could say anything more.

The hired gun finished his drink, pulled on his coat, and locked the room carefully behind him. Downstairs, he tossed a quarter to a bellboy to bring his horse up and waited on the porch.

Thirty minutes later he was sitting in Agnew's study, sipping a glass of imported whiskey and listening casually to the rancher.

'How long?' Agnew came straight to the point. 'You been sightseeing for two days now.'

'I've been watching Cade.' Klein's voice prompted Agnew to replenish his own glass. 'You said you wanted it quiet, so I need to study his habits.'

'I'm paying five thousand dollars for a bullet,' rasped Agnew, irritation flushing his florid face. 'All you have to do is put it in the right place.'

Klein shook his head, red eyes boring into his employer. 'You're paying five thousand for my expertise. Any fool can trigger a gun. If you ain't particular about how Cade gets it, I can take him tonight.'

17

'Don't mince around.' Agnew smoothed the thinning remnants of his hair. 'You know how to do it. I don't want the boy hurt and I don't want my name linked to the killing. It's Cade I want in boot hill. But when? When you planning to do it?'

Klein smiled slowly, sipping his drink.

'You set a whole pack o' conditions on this thing,' he murmured. 'The kind that makes it difficult for a man to get his work done. How come you're so almighty fussy? What's it matter if the kid gets killed too?'

Agnew started, colour draining from his face. His hands clenched tight, knuckles whitening under the pressure, and a low, strangled moan broke from his gaping mouth.

'No! You hear me, Klein? No!'

'I think,' said Klein evenly, 'that you better do a little explainin'.'

'I gave my word,' Agnew mumbled, and for a moment his face lost its hard-edged look, an old sadness filling his eyes. 'To my wife.'

'She's dead,' said Klein bluntly.

'Yeah.' Agnew took a long swallow, remembering. 'Thanks to Cade. Was him caused her death. But Gloria – that was her name – she took a real fancy to the boy. Our son died young an' she wanted to adopt Andy Prescott. Cade fought me over it. The gun went off. Gloria died.' His eyes were empty now. 'But I gave my word that I wouldn't harm the kid. That still stands, Klein: you don't touch the boy. Get Cade, but don't hurt Andy.'

Klein nodded, letting random thoughts drift through his mind. Somewhere in here there might just be the makings of a lot more than five thousand dollars. Agnew had money, that was sure. It was evident in the big house and the liveried servants hanging around it. Even more in the gossip he had picked up around town. Agnew's interests stretched way beyond ranching – which alone accounted for a large part of his wealth – into the banks and shipping lines, railroads, manufacturing. A man with that kind of money was worth getting to know. He grinned, emptying his glass.

'All right. I'll take Cade tomorrow or the day after. The kid won't be hurt.'

Agnew inclined his head without speaking and Klein wondered if it was a tear glinting on his cheek. The gunman wasted little time on the contemplation: he had little to spare for men too thin-spined to do their own killing.

'I'll head out pretty soon after. You won't hear from me, except to know he's done for.'

He wasted no time on good-byes, just stood up and walked out of the room. Behind him, Agnew sat staring into space, his mind filled with a face glamourized by the passage of time. The face of his dead wife.

Within the shabby confines of the Denver House, Jubal Cade shared a similar memory. His own wife had died under the gun of the same outlaw who had blinded Andy. Since then he had come up against the man twice, once in Texas,* and once in Arizona.* The killer had escaped on both occasions, leaving Jubal further embittered. Now, as he looked around the sparse furnishings of the room, he wondered if he would ever achieve his original goal.

Jubal Cade was a doctor, trained in England, where he had met and married Mary, but it was a long time – too long – since he had practised medicine. He still carried his valise of instruments and medicaments, but more familiar now was the feel of the .30 calibre Spencer rifle or the Merwin & Hulbert revolver shoulder-holstered beneath his left arm. A medical practice was, now, a half-forgotten dream left over from the good years. More pressing was the need to provide three hundred dollars a month to keep Andy in the Lenz Clinic. So far Jubal had succeeded, though it was a constant, nagging worry that drove him far across the open spaces of America to find the money. The last few days in St. Louis had yielded a good return, close on nine hundred dollars coming in from his poker winnings. But soon he would have to quit the place in search of fresh funds.

* See: Jubal Cade – *Killer Silver* and *The Golden Dead*.

With that unwelcome thought in mind he settled down to sleep.

Morning dawned clear and sultry, the rising sun lighting the turgid waters of the Mississippi with a golden luminescence. Jubal woke with the light, conscious of the heat already boring into the small room. At two dollars a day, all found, it was cheap enough, but he wished the windows faced some direction other than east. Yawning, he swung his feet off the bed and splashed water over his face. After breakfast he planned to ride out to the clinic again and spend the day with Andy before turning over his poker winnings to Lenz to guarantee the boy a few more months under the professor's care. It was an expensive operation, but Lenz ran the only school-cum-hospital for blind people in a thousand miles. And it was the best this side of Washington. The curriculum centred on teaching blind people to cope with their affliction while seeking a cure at the same time. In Andy's case, hopes ran high. The bullet that had robbed him of his sight had done no permanent damage: its passage through his forehead had not touched the optic nerves, though the impact – or perhaps the nervous shock – had rendered the youngster sightless to the extent that he could now discern vague outlines at no more than a few feet. One operation, financed by reward money on a Kluxer, had failed.* Jubal wondered if Lenz would contemplate a second.

His face, as he entered the Denver House's restaurant, was dour.

The room, even though it was little more than an hour past dawn, was busy and Jubal was forced to join several other guests at one of the big tables. He ignored their conversation as he drank the bitter coffee, focusing his attention on the ham and eggs set before him. The Denver House was no great shakes as a hotel, but the food was pretty good and surprisingly plentiful. Afterwards, he lit a cheroot and moved out to the boardwalk, settling into a chair while he smoked, watching the city come to life.

* See: Jubal Cade – *The Burning Man.*

Farther up the street, still relatively quiet at this time of day, Saul Klein set match to corncob and puffed contentedly as he watched his target. Cade would finish the cheroot before fetching his horse from the nearby livery stable. After that he would saddle up and ride out to the Lenz Clinic to see the boy. They would spend the day together before Cade headed back to the centre of town for dinner and cards in one of the saloons. So far Klein had followed him into three, the Silver Dollar, the Cattleman's Rest, and the Creole Empire. Any one of the trio would serve the gunman's purpose as well as the open road; it was a decision he could take later, immediately prior to Cade's death.

Unaware of the scrutiny, Jubal finished the cheroot and flicked the stub into the dust of the roadway. He climbed to his feet and stretched lazily before walking over to the stable. He saddled the big bay he was using and then, almost as an afterthought, rode the horse back down the street to the Denver House. Soft St. Louis living was making him absent-minded: he had left the Spencer in his room.

The rifle secured in the saddle sheath, he turned the bay round and headed out towards the clinic. He took his time, giving Andy a chance to eat breakfast and get cleaned up before he arrived. Professor Lenz liked to maintain a fixed routine which not even paying customers were permitted to disrupt, so Jubal timed his visits carefully to avoid upsetting the irascible German doctor. The bay chose its own pace, dawdling through the sunlight so that the gold Hunter slung across Jubal's vest showed eight o'clock as they walked through the impressive gates opening onto the frontal lawns of the place. Jubal climbed down in front of the main building, handing his reins to the smiling negro who appeared at the door.

The age-lined face creased as he saw the rider, and there was extra warmth in his mellow voice as he greeted the visitor.

'Mistuh Cade. It's good to see you, suh. Young Andy's waitin' on you inside.'

'Thanks, Caleb.' Jubal brushed road dust from his suit as he spoke. 'I'll get on in.'

'He sure looks forwards to seein' you, mistuh Cade,' grinned the servant. 'Can't hardly talk of nuthin' else.'

Jubal smiled, the expression lifting years from his face, and waved good-bye as he climbed the steps. He pushed through the big doors into the cool interior of the hall, pausing to let his eyes adjust to the dimness inside. His tread was soft, habitually light, but to the boy waiting on a bench across the room it was like a shout of greeting.

'Jubal!' Andy Prescott came out of his seat like a tousled-haired cannonball. 'What we gonna do today?'

'Maybe,' grinned Jubal, 'we should spend some time teaching you not to say *gonna*.'

'Shucks, Jubal, I'm sorry.' Andy's lapses into bad grammar were a constant source of amusement to them both. Try as he might, the youngster was unable to shake the habit. 'But like paw always said: it's the deeds that count, not the words.'

'Yeah,' said Jubal, mock-serious, 'but if actions speak louder than words, you'd best make both clear.'

For a moment Andy looked crestfallen at his slip, but then his natural good humour asserted itself and he grinned, thrusting out his right hand.

'It's still good to see you.'

Jubal's smile was tinged with sadness as he heard the greeting, Andy's unconscious reference reminding him of the boy's plight. He shook the hand solemnly, thinking that it wasn't very long ago that Andy had been ten years old and more likely to greet him with open arms than a formal handshake. Still, he reminded himself, kids grew up fast and Andy was rapidly approaching adolescence. He looked down at the sightless blue eyes, noting that they were closer to the level of his own than he recalled, and squeezed the boy's hand.

'Thought we might talk the professor into loaning us a rig and drive up the river a way.'

'That'd be fun.' Andy was immediately enthusiastic. 'I like the smell of summer.'

Jubal ruffled his hair and followed the youngster's tugging hand towards the professor's study. By now, Andy could find his way around the clinic as well as any sighted person, and his refusal to let his blindness depress him made Jubal proud.

Later, seated on the bench of the spring wagon, he was amazed at the boy's receptiveness. It was as though the loss of his sight had resulted in a heightening of Andy's other faculties. His hearing was acute, his movements deft and sure, and he seemed to have developed a sixth sense that told him when someone was nearby, or even what his immediate companion was thinking.

That sense marred their day.

Jubal took the rig northwards, following the bank of the river, taking things easy as Andy rambled on about his lessons and the progress he was making. Erich Lenz had already suggested to Jubal that another operation might be in order soon, but that first he would like Andy to take a vacation, somewhere hot and dry where he could relax and build his strength. The only likely place Jubal could think of was Virginia Cantrell's ranch in Texas, and as yet he was wary of going back there.* Equally, the money was a problem: the operation would be expensive and he had no idea where he would find it. Such doubts did not worry Andy; but something else did.

They halted at noon by a lonely roadhouse where the owner's wife fussed over the blind boy until he turned to Jubal and demanded, in a loud whisper, to know why he should be the object of so much attention.

'She's trying to be kind, Andy,' murmured Jubal.

'You mean she feels sorry for me.' It was the first hint of bitterness Jubal had heard. 'Because I can't see.'

'She means well, son,' said Jubal, softly.

'Lotta folks mean well,' Andy rejoined. 'Trouble is, they don't know what it's like being blind.'

There was nothing Jubal could say, so instead he simply reached to squeeze the boy's hand. Andy returned the pressure and after a moment began to smile again.

'I don't mean you, Jubal. I know you understand. And any-

* See: Jubal Cade – *Days of Blood*.

way,' his voice took on a defiant note, 'I'm gonna see again.'

'*Going to*,' corrected Jubal, automatically.

Andy chuckled. 'Sorry, Jubal. I try to get it right, honest.'

The moment of bitterness passed and they settled down to eat. The woman's cooking matched her intentions with more favourable results, and they left the roadhouse with tight belts and a feeling of well-being. Until Andy's sixth sense came into play.

'There any riders about?' He asked almost casually.

Jubal glanced around: the countryside was empty.

'Someone's close by,' Andy said with total conviction. 'I can feel them.'

'I don't see anyone,' Jubal answered. 'The road's been clear for the past hour.'

'Someone's watching us.' Andy was definite.

'Could be someone's out hunting.' Jubal was unaware of anyone in the vicinity, but none the less prepared to trust the boy's instinct. 'Maybe in the brush.'

'No.' Andy shook his head. 'I can feel someone watching us. If they was hunting we'd have heard shots.'

Jubal shrugged. 'It's close on suppertime anyway. We'll head back, could be we'll spot them on the way.'

Andy said nothing; but he shivered suddenly, as though a chill wind brushed over him. During the return journey he remained silent, head cocked to one side in a listening position.

Saul Klein watched them go from the cover of a canebrake. It had been a long, hot day, and boring too. He was a naturally patient man – had to be in his line of work – but Cade's routine was beginning to irritate him. He had promised Agnew that the killing would take place soon and now he figured that he knew enough about Cade's habits to fulfil his contract and ride clear. It was the boy who interested him now, and for that reason alone he had spent a day skulking under cover with sweat plastering his shirt to his ribs. Swearing softly, he mounted his horse and began to follow the spring wagon from the farther side of the sheltering cane.

He stayed a quarter-mile back until they reached the clinic. Then he waited until the rig disappeared through the gates and moved over onto the road. He kicked his stallion to a fast canter, going by the gates in a swirl of dust that hid him from any possible watchers. Half a mile down the road he reined in and turned the big black off into the brush. A wild apple thicket provided the cover he sought, and he tethered the horse to one of the stubby trees. Gently, he tied a bandanna around the animal's nostrils to shut off involuntary sounds, and lifted a rifle from the saddle scabbard.

It was the Winchester 1873, a standard model but for the load and the sights. The bullets in the chamber were made to Klein's personal specification, carrying a quarter more powder grains than was normal; the sights were completely rebuilt to incorporate a small telescope shipped in from Germany. Klein carried the sniper's gun with care as he settled down amongst the scrubby trees, aligning the cross-hairs on the road below.

Jubal dismissed Andy's worry as he rode away from the Lenz Clinic. The youngster had remained doubtful right up to their parting, but the thought of supper and Jubal's promise to come by again the next day had gone a long way to cheering him up. Jubal kept his eyes open as he rode away, but by now he was fairly sure that Andy's premonition had been based on some lonely hunter settled into the cane flanking the river.

He held the bay to a steady trot as he followed the road back into St. Louis. Part of his mind enjoyed the magnificent spectacle of the sun going down beyond the city, bathing the Mississippi in fiery red light; another part dwelt on Lenz's parting words.

'The operation must be soon. The boy is growing fast, and the longer he remains without his sight, the less able he becomes to cope if he regains it. I realize your problems, Doctor Cade; but we must act soon. Please try to find the money.'

It was, Jubal mused, easier said than done. Lenz was talking about three thousand dollars: a whole lot more than Jubal could lay hands on right now.

25

He was still worrying about it when he rode into Saul Klein's specially built rifle sights.

The gunman was squatting beside a wild apple tree, the Winchester cradled against his right shoulder, his elbows resting firmly on his knees. He trailed Jubal for a moment, lining the sights on the centre of the grey coat, mildly irritated that the sun was shining on his face. Then he squeezed the trigger and felt the familiar thud of the stock against his shoulder.

And laughed as his target pitched sideways off the bay horse.

CHAPTER THREE

Jubal felt a terrific blow smash into his ribs. Pain lanced fiery barbs through his stomach and chest, and a wave of nausea clouded his vision. He was dimly aware of the bay horse rearing up, but then a great roaring sound filled his ears and sparks danced over his eyes. A second blow gusted air from his lungs and the sun went out abruptly as a quenched match. Jubal tasted the salt tang of blood in his mouth and gave himself up to the darkness.

Saul Klein watched the body for a moment. It was face down in the dust of the road, a dark stain spreading slowly beneath the left arm. Immediately below the body, the dust was growing thick, muddy, as blood dripped steadily from the wound.

The man from Salt Lake City spread his thin lips in a smile: he liked to do a job well.

Moving fast, he slid the Winchester back into the sheath, pulled the bandanna from the stallion's nostrils, and mounted. He rode away without looking back, moving through the scrub hedging the road until he was a clear mile from the corpse. Then he moved back to the track and heeled the animal to a canter, heading for Agnew's place.

The rancher met him in the study. It was a comfortable, thick-carpeted room, the walls lined with books that looked as though they got less attention than the decanters set on a mahogany table close by Agnew's desk. Klein stared meaningfully at the cut crystal, settling into a brocade armchair as Agnew poured two stiff measures of the good whiskey.

'Well?' The man's voice was paused midway between irritation and hope: Klein's visit had caught him in the middle of supper. 'You got anything new to tell me?'

'Yeah.' Klein's pallid face was waxen in the soft glow of

27

dollars.'

Agnew started, choking on his drink.

'You mean you done it? You killed him?'

Klein nodded, smiling.

'The boy? You didn't touch the boy?'

Klein shook his head. 'No. Cade dropped him at the clinic. I laid up for Cade on the road back. He's most like still there.'

Agnew inclined his balding head without speaking. He set his whiskey down on the desk, the nervous trembling of his hand spilling a ring of liquor over the polished wood. Still silent, he opened a drawer and took out a key. Crossing to the far wall, he knelt down to open a safe, reaching inside. When he stood up he was holding a sheaf of notes. He went back behind the desk and placed the money carefully on the farther edge. Klein stared at the wad for a moment, finishing his drink, then picked it up and stuffed it inside his black coat.

'You don't want to count it?' Agnew sounded vaguely surprised.

'I don't think you'd try to cheat me.' Klein's voice was soft, flat. 'If you do I'll come back.'

Agnew shivered, staring at the albino. After a while he looked away from the red eyes, fighting hard to quell the fear that was threatening to spill his dinner, and drained his glass in one nervous gulp.

Klein smiled again, enjoying the rancher's discomfort. Then he turned and walked to the door.

'I'll be around St. Louis a while longer. If we meet up, you don't know me: it's safer that way.'

Agnew nodded, waiting until the door closed behind the gunman before he poured his glass brimful and sank uneasily into his chair. For long moments he sat without moving, then he took a deep breath, swallowed whiskey, and opened a drawer. He extracted a sheaf of papers, thumbing through them with a familiarity that suggested they had been read

28

many times before. The essential details were all filled in, with the exception of two vital sections: the date and the signature of the county magistrate. The papers were adoption forms, the name at their head was Andrew Prescott.

He glanced up at the two portraits hung above the fireplace. One showed a snub-nosed boy with unruly hair and wide eyes, bearing a remarkable resemblance to Andy: it was a portrait of Agnew's dead son. The second was of a woman, slender and blonde, who had once been delicately beautiful, but – even to the artist – appeared haunted, lost.

'Gloria.' Agnew's voice was a thick mumble as he stared at the face of his dead wife. 'I done it. Just like I promised. Cade dead and the boy ours.'

Solemnly, he lifted his glass in a toast to the deceased.

'Andrew Curtis Agnew. That's what I'll call him, honey. He'll forget Cade in time, an' I'll ship every goddam surgeon in the United States to St. Louis to get his sight back.'

He set his glass down and dragged a hand over his eyes, wiping away the tears. Then, fortifying himself with a third, long swallow, he reached for a bell rope.

Moments later, a negro manservant came through the door, his dark face impassive, his voice neutral.

'Your visitor has gone, sir. Shall I serve a fresh dinner?'

'No. No.' Agnew shook his head, a smile beginning to form on his fleshy lips. 'Send someone for Laurence. He won't be in his office now, so tell them to try the St. Charles House, or the Chartrain. If he's not there, find him. I want him now.'

The servant murmured something, backing from the room. A short while later Agnew heard horse hooves pound away into the night.

Sydney Laurence arrived one and a half hours later, his lank black hair plastered over his shoulders by the ride through the warm night, his dark suit more disreputable than ever. He came into the study with his gold-framed spectacles in one hand, a grubby kerchief in the other. Agnew watched him, surprised – despite their long relationship – that the scruffy lawyer was still the finest legal brain in five states.

He called for coffee, gave the man whiskey, and outlined his plans.

It was close on midnight before they were finished, but by that time Agnew was confident of adopting Andy. Laurence would confront Judge Harvey with the papers come morning; backed by Agnew's money and his standing in the St. Louis community it was a foregone conclusion that the orphan would be signed over to Ben Agnew. The 'accidental' discovery of Jubal Cade's corpse would serve only to emphasize the need for a wealthy step-parent.

Agnew was happy with Laurence's advice.

Saul Klein was happy with the money Agnew had given him; it was a tidy base for the next part of the plan that had formed since shooting Cade. The part that would pull in more of Agnew's money.

Jubal Cade was hurting. Hurting bad. Klein's first bullet had hit directly below his left armpit. The heavy-grained slug had torn through the cloth of his jacket like a knife through sun-melted butter. Then it had hit the Merwin & Hulbert slung under his left arm. The lead slug had spread out on impact, splattering against the steel cylinder of the revolver with sufficient force to detonate several of the cartridges. The blast, concentrated through the closed chambers, had opened a gaping wound in his side. Two – perhaps more – ribs were broken, and he was losing a great deal of blood.

The second shot had clipped his shoulder as he tumbled from the stampeded horse. It was, he guessed, no more than a flesh wound, more painful than serious.

At the moment, as he breathed dust in from the road, either one of the wounds could kill him. Slowly, horribly conscious of the pain in his left side, he shifted his right arm across to test the size of the wound. It seemed to spread across most of his chest, presumably from lacerations caused by the fragmenting revolver, and down from his armpit to his waist. He could no longer feel his left arm, though the drip of blood told him of the flesh wound. He realized that he was unable to use the left side of his body. And at the same time knew that he must find help fast, or bleed to death in the sticky dust of the road.

Jubal Cade was a small man, no more than five feet six inches, but packed solid with muscle honed fine by danger. He opened his eyes and realized that he was still alive, dragged his aching right arm up under his body, and pushed, lifting himself off the road.

It hurt like hell, but he turned over, getting his mouth out of the dirt, and sucked in long, heady lungfuls of air. He rested on his back until he felt capable of making another move. Then he hiked his knees up, slung his right arm around his braced legs, and hauled his torso to a sitting position. When he breathed, blood came out of his mouth, but he ignored it. He set both arms on the ground and tried to push himself up.

He screamed when the pressure hit his left side, and tumbled back, fainting.

Some time later he came to again and hunched his legs beneath his body, drawing them tight against the pain in his chest. He braced his good arm on the ground and fought his way upwards, choking on the blood that flooded into his mouth. He had no idea how long it took, but finally he got onto his feet, staggering as the night spun madly around his foggy eyes. He wasn't even sure which direction he was headed, but he set one foot in front of the other and forced his body to walk.

His left arm hung limp down his side, sticky with spilled blood; the right was held tight against his left ribs in an effort to compress the pain and staunch the pulsing flow of blood that threatened to drain his life away.

Each step was agony, the jar of his boots against the roadway shuddering pain through his body. He could see no more than a few feet ahead, and red mists swirled madly across his eyes. He realized that he was sweating badly, and diagnosed – with instinctive concern born of his medical training – that he was suffering from shock. He knew that he would die before very long. It was a solid, scientific fact: no one could sustain the injuries he had taken, the loss of blood, and live.

31

His only chance was to keep moving – which, in itself, meant a greater loss of blood – in the hope that he could reach some place that could help.

He clenched his teeth tight against the pain and concentrated on walking.

Saul Klein had an easier journey. He left Agnew's palatial home on the black stallion and rode slowly into the centre of St. Louis. As yet, his plan was unformed in its specific details and he wanted time to work out the necessary angles. With Cade gone the thing could wait anyway; Agnew would have no chance of acting for at least twelve hours, and by then it could all be done.

The man from Salt Lake City checked out of his hotel, stashed his gear on the stallion, and headed back towards the Lenz Clinic.

He reached the place about the same time that Sydney Laurence got to Agnew's spread, just as Jubal Cade was pushing himself up from the dirt. He skirted the high stone walls, heading down to the river where the walls gave way to rolling grassland that afforded him an easy entrance. He left his horse hitched to a tall oak tree close by the wall. It was hidden from view by the shadows of the tree and the stone, and no one saw him approach the house.

He found an open window and slipped inside. Tiptoeing over the floorboards, he moved to the nearest door: the space inside was silent. He eased the door open and drifted through, a pale shadow in the dim hallway. Up ahead was a drowsing man, slumped into the confines of a velveteen armchair. Klein came up behind the man without a sound. His right arm slid around the throat, jerking the head back as his left hand settled over the mouth.

'You make one single sound and you're dead.' He applied pressure to the man's neck and skull as he said it. 'So you just listen an' give the right answers, an' that way you might stay alive.'

Under the paralysing grip the negro simply nodded, his eyes wide with fear and shock.

32

'Good,' whispered Klein, 'you might live long enough to be buried. Where's Andy Prescott?'

The servant grunted, his eyes flashing in the direction of the relevant dormitory. Klein noted the glance, and hauled the man to his feet, propelling him across the floor with an outthrust knee. They came to one of the ground floor dormitories and the negro bobbed his head in agitated indication. Klein said nothing, just grinned as he tightened his grip around the windpipe and shifted the pressure of his left hand from the man's mouth to the side of his head. He leaned back, lifting the servant's feet clear of the floor. He held the man there until he heard the heavy *click* of separating vertebrae, and felt the head sag sideways. For a moment longer he held the body upright, waiting for the legs to go still, then lowered it to the floor on one side of the door.

In death the negro looked smaller, as though the sudden extinction of his life had drained something physical from his body.

Klein ignored the corpse as he opened the door.

He went through with the Smith & Wesson cocked in his hand, squinting his blood-stained eyes into the darkness. The boys were coming awake, alert to the sudden sounds, and he grabbed the nearest, shoving the revolver's muzzle up against the youngster's cheek.

'Andy Prescott. Where is he?'

The child shrank back from the cold metal and Klein jammed it harder against the flesh, grinding the end down to drive skin painfully against teeth.

'Three beds down ...' The answer was close to tears. 'My side. Don't kill me mister ... please ...'

Klein grunted, and clipped the child along his temple with the barrel, letting him fall back unconscious as he hurried to Andy's bunk.

The fair-haired boy was sitting up in bed, a startled expression wiping the sleep from his face. He cocked his head to one side, listening to the gunman's soft-footed approach.

'Who is it?' He sounded nervous, sensing danger.

33

'You an' me are taking a ride,' grunted Klein.

He slapped a hand tight over Andy's mouth, lifting the struggling youngster from the bed. 'One yelp an' I'll lay you out. Understand?'

Andy nodded, mumbling around the gagging hand. 'You better watch out, Mister. Jubal Cade's gonna be coming after you.'

Klein chuckled. 'Don't count on that. Your friend is napping, kid.'

CHAPTER FOUR

Jubal could feel blood oozing stickily between his fingers. His legs felt like the bones had been removed, and each breath seemed to suck fire through his lungs, spinning his head while a kettledrum beat a loud tattoo inside his skull. He lost count of the times he fell down, and when he saw the lights he was crawling awkwardly through the dust.

It was hard to tell, through the haze of pain, whether the lights were real, or products of his waning consciousness, but he pushed his torn body towards them anyway. The roughness of a stone pillar informed him of their reality, and he pushed feebly against the wrought iron gates hung from the stone. The gates swung open on oiled hinges and he fell through. At the farther end of a gravelled driveway, lights burned bright in a large building where people seemed to be running around in panic. Feverishly, Jubal wondered how they could have known he was coming, then realized the confusion must be caused by some other event.

He heard the pounding of a fast-driven horse and tried to call out as a big black stallion went down the road at full gallop. The rider was too busy holding a struggling figure across the saddle to notice the man sprawled in the drive, so Jubal concentrated on reaching the house.

It was oddly familiar, but he couldn't quite place it as he dragged himself to his feet again and tottered towards the lights. The outline of the building kept shifting, wavering as he staggered doggedly along the avenue. The shouting seemed to come from a great distance away, approaching and receding like waves breaking against the ravaged shore of his mind. Then he came to the steps and lifted one foot onto the first wide platform. The effort was too much and he pitched forwards, crashing heavily against scrubbed stone. The shouting stopped and he felt hands touch him, turn him on his back. Then, a familiar voice he couldn't recognize.

'My God! It's Dr. Cade.'

A lantern was brought and Jubal forced himself to concentrate his vision through the flickering waves of pain. He saw a round, smooth-skinned face, almost cherubic beneath the dome of the hairless skull, and grinned.

'Evening, professor.'

The face belonged to Erich Lenz.

When he came to again he couldn't remember where he was. The room was small and spotlessly clean, a tall window allowing a shaft of sunlight to enter from between heavy drapes. It illuminated a heavy, expensive-looking bureau, the rich colour of well-polished mahogany attesting to the presence of money. It lit a wall covered with some costly, gold-striped paper, and an oil painting depicting a calm, pastoral scene. The room was very quiet, only the steady buzzing of a fly disturbing the silence. Slowly, aware of pain along his side and shoulder, Jubal turned his head. The buzzing came, not from a fly, but the negro dozing in a chair alongside the bed. Jubal squinted, trying to recall the face, then recognized Caleb, Lenz's head footman. He opened his mouth, forming the man's name, but no words came out, only a dry, rasping sound.

It was enough to wake the old man. He sat up with a start, a huge grin splitting his face when he saw Jubal watching him.

'Mistuh Cade, sir! We thought you was done for.' He sounded happy that the diagnosis had proved wrong. 'You come in all bloody and shot. Lawd, what a night that was.'

Jubal tried to ask a question, but his throat was too dry and the words seemed to clog in great lumps halfway down his windpipe. Caleb, still smiling, reached behind him, producing a moistened flannel that he touched to Jubal's lips.

'Now don't you go tryin' to talk, sir. Strict orders of the professor. You just lay still while I go fetch him.'

He re-arranged the pillows and left the room in a hurry, returning moments later with Lenz. The little German eye

36

specialist came into the room with worry putting lines into his youthful skin and his hands fidgeting nervously around the watch tucked into his vest pocket. Weak though he was, Jubal was surprised by the man's appearance. Lenz was normally the most self-asssured man Jubal had ever met, a massive share of self-confidence rendering him almost aloof to worry, a dispassionate healer of the sick, too sure of his own skills to permit their suffering to disturb him.

Now, though, he seemed almost distraught. Jubal wondered why.

'Dr. Cade.' Lenz sat down as he spoke, checking Jubal's pulse with automatic precision. 'How do you feel?'

'Rotten,' answered Jubal, frankly. 'How bad am I hurt?'

'Enough,' murmured Lenz, professional objectivity overriding his worry. 'To be honest, I am surprised that you survived. Most men would have bled to death, numbed by the shock. So far as we have been able to ascertain, you were shot from your horse a half-mile from here. You walked – or crawled – back. In some ways you were extremely lucky: that gun you keep on your left side took the impact of the first bullet. The shot, however, while failing to penetrate your body, exploded the pistol so that fragments of steel imbedded in your side. Two ribs broke, and a large wound was opened. Several cartridges detonated, resulting in severe flash burns along your left hip.'

He broke off, carefully lifting the sheets to study the dressings circling Jubal's body. Then continued.

'A second bullet entered your left shoulder. Presumably you were falling from your horse, angling your body away from the direct line of the shot. It entered above the collar bone, which deflected it upwards to cause only a bad flesh wound. Had it penetrated the bone and the muscle, you would have lost the use of your left arm.' He grunted approvingly, settling the sheets back over Jubal's supine form. 'You are a lucky man, Dr. Cade. You should be dead.'

'Like it says in the Bible,' whispered Jubal thickly, 'physician, heal thyself. Or find help fast.'

'You were lucky,' said Lenz seriously. 'And very strong. Few men could have made that journey. As it was, you have been unconscious for three days.'

'Three days!' Jubal was surprised despite his own medical training. 'You told Andy? He was expecting me back.'

Lenz shook his head slowly, starting to fidget with the watch again. Then he composed himself and looked straight into Jubal's eyes.

'No, Dr. Cade, I have not told Andy. The boy is not here. Shortly before you arrived someone broke into the clinic. A solitary man, by all accounts. He killed my night watchman and took Andy Prescott with him. Why, I cannot imagine; but the boy is gone. I have informed the marshal, of course, and he is now seeking the kidnapper. I know nothing else. There has been no ransom note, no word of any kind. I took it upon myself to post a reward of five hundred dollars, but so far nothing has come of it. All we can do is wait.'

'Like hell,' Jubal started to say, but Lenz reached over, deftly inserting a hypodermic in his arm as he pushed up from the bed.

The morphine acted fast on Jubal's weakened system and he sank back against the pillows with a feeling of sleepy well-being fighting the frustration and anger. Against his will, he felt his eyes closing as the darkness rolled back over his mind. As he lost consciousness again, his own words came to him: *Physician, heal thyself.* But this time, do it fast!

While Jubal Cade fought to stay alive in the Lenz Clinic, Ben Agnew fought raw anger. Sydney Laurence had presented the adoption papers to Judge Harvey on schedule, but Cade's body had failed to show up as planned. Discreet investigations by Agnew men had produced Cade's horse – currently held by the law – with blood on the saddle. There was more blood on the road into St. Louis, a great deal; but no body to go with it. So Harvey refused to sign the papers. The bearded, balding judge was loath to offend Agnew, but held closer still to the letter of the law: no proof of Cade's demise meant no grounds for readoption. Then word came in of Cade's condition.

Agnew cursed volubly and at great length when he heard the man was still alive. He set Laurence to checking legal precedents for establishing Cade's unfitness to foster Andy. And then he got the greater shock: Andy Prescott had disappeared. His first assumption was that Jubal had hidden the boy, but that was patently impossible, given Jubal's condition.

The explanation came in a telegraph from Angel, Kansas. It was stated in terms that would not implicate the sender without incriminating Agnew alongside; but the rancher knew exactly what it meant. And didn't like it.

The message read: ANDY WELL AND ENJOYING TRIP. WILL NEED EXTRA MONEY FOR VACATION. RETURN FARE EXPENSIVE. $15,000. SEND REPLY TO THIS OFFICE.

It was signed: KLEIN.

Agnew acted immediately. First, he wired a reply agreeing to the price and asking where he should collect Andy. He did not trust the gunman to return the boy alive any more than he expected Klein to trust him, but it didn't hurt to cover all the angles. Second, he wired Chicago, demanding that Allan Pinkerton send his best man immediately – price no problem – to follow the trail.

The Pinkerton man arrived four days later, tired by a long ride up from Louisiana, but still professionally keen to take the case. He was a middle-aged investigator, a thatch of dark hair fading into grey, though the eyes remained keen and clearly blue. Agnew outlined the events of the past week, leaving out the part about hiring Klein to kill Jubal Cade. The story Elias Holden ended up with was that Agnew had planned to hire Saul Klein as a Range Detective – that seemed to cover the possibility of them having been seen together – but that the albino had disappeared, gone under cover until the wire arrived from Angel.

Holden had been too long with the Pinkerton Agency to accept the story at face value. The sweat beading Agnew's face and hands was more than would be normal for a man worried about a relatively unknown boy, and whenever Klein's name was mentioned, the rancher's left eye developed an ugly tic. But the Pinkerton was promised a hefty reward on top of his wages if he found the kidnapper and brought Andy Prescott back alive, so he stilled his doubts and set about finding a trail to follow. Angel seemed the logical place to start, and he bought a ticket on the Kansas Pacific, heading westwards through Missouri in the direction of the little tank town that was his only lead to Andy Prescott.

While Holden discussed his plans with Agnew, Jubal was regaining his strength faster than normal in the Lenz Clinic.

Professor Lenz, although specializing in eye surgery, was still an excellent all-round doctor. He had successfully extracted splinters of exploded metal from Jubal's side, bound up the broken ribs, and sealed off the open wounds. After that, it was a question of time and rest before the wiry body healed enough to be active again. For long, frustrating days Jubal gathered strength under the morphine, sipping broth when he woke, mending slowly while his mind raced ahead of his body. He ignored Lenz's instructions to rest and climbed out of bed after a week. Within two, he was talking about leaving the clinic and setting out to look for Andy.

Lenz did his best to dissuade him.

'Dr. Cade,' he said patiently, 'you are still sick. You know that as well as I. Would you permit a patient with your wounds out of bed so soon?'

Jubal shook his head. 'Guess not, Professor. But then again, I couldn't stop them if they wanted to. And I do have other problems.'

Lenz snorted his irritation. 'What can you do for Andy that is not done already? The marshal has sent word out. I have posted a reward. Ben Agnew has hired the Pinkertons to find the child.'

'Agnew?' Jubal started up from the bench in the warm garden. 'What's he got to do with this?'

'How should I know?' Lenz shrugged. 'I can only quote

40

what I've heard around town. It appears that Mr. Agnew has hired a Pinkerton detective to locate Andy. The Pinkertons, I understand, are very good at that kind of thing. What can you do that they can't?'

Jubal didn't answer. He was thinking too hard about the connections. He let Lenz persuade him back to his room and waited until the peppery little German was gone before getting dressed and sliding the window up. His grey suit had been patched and cleaned, though it was long overdue for replacement, and he would need a new handgun. Lenz had told him his horse was stabled near the marshal's office, so he penned a brief note before he left, explaining that he was borrowing a mount for the journey into St. Louis that could be collected from the marshal's office.

He found a skewbald gelding in the stables behind the clinic, and a saddle in the tackroom. An hour later, with his side on fire, he was in the marshal's office.

They recognized him, and agreed to return the professor's horse. A deputy even offered to carry Jubal's gear down to the stable and explain that the bay horse was to be released. Jubal was grateful: his wounds were hurting from the ride in and the night looked to be busy. First on his programme was the acquisition of a new handgun, which he found in the nearest hardware store. With little time to waste on the niceties of ballistics, he purchased a standard model Colt .45, the short-barrel Peacemaker. It was slower to load than the ruined Merwin & Hulbert, and rather less accurate, but it could be replaced almost anywhere in the West, and the necessary cartridges were available from a myriad stores all over America. He also bought three cartons of .30 calibre shells for the Spencer rifle, a pack of cheroots, and two bottles of whiskey. The latter was a poor anaesthetic, but it would numb his pain and allow him to stay awake longer than morphine.

After that he mounted up and rode out to Agnew's place.

The house was in darkness, except for one lighted window that Jubal could see from the road. He swung down off the

41

bay horse and tethered the big animal to a bougainvillaea. The horse cropped grass as Jubal slipped through the shadows, making for the light.

He fetched up against the side of the house and moved quietly alongside the glass. The drapes were back and he could see Agnew sitting behind a wide desk, drinking whiskey and looking angry. He recognized the room from his first visit to the place: this was where Gloria Agnew had died, an accidental victim of the rancher's ambition. He smiled slowly, the gesture emphasizing the scar tissue across the bridge of his nose, and drew the Colt.

Gently he rapped on the windowpane, holding to the shadows. Agnew looked up, frowning at the unexpected sound. Jubal tapped again, watching the rancher rise with an irritable motion. Either Agnew was too drunk to worry, or was accustomed to clandestine visits; either way, he crossed the room and opened the windows.

The full-length panes of glass opened inwards, and as they swung back Jubal went through the gap. Agnew staggered as the muzzle of the Colt drove hard into his spreading belly, then tripped and measured his length on the carpet with a solid *thud*. Jubal kicked the windows shut with his heel, keeping the Peacemaker levelled on Agnew's chest. The rancher puffed, blowing a cloud of whiskey-tainted breath upwards, and shook his head, trying to focus his eyes on the intruder. When he recognized the man, he gaped, his fleshy face growing abruptly red, then pale.

Jubal grinned, though there was no friendship in the look. 'You got things to tell me, Agnew.'

He hauled the hammer of the Colt back, the double *click* unnaturally loud in the sudden stillness.

'I thought you was sick.' Agnew's voice was throaty with a mixture of fear and whiskey. 'They told me you was laid up in the clinic.'

'Past tense is right,' grated Jubal. 'But I discharged myself. Your man missed it, Agnew. Next time hire a better gun.'

It was a long shot, based on pure guesswork and the fact

that Andy had been taken the same night Jubal was shot. But it worked.

'He was the best.' Maybe, had Agnew consumed less alcohol, he might not have said it. Once out, he realized that he was committed, and opted to brazen it out. 'You knew I'd get you, Cade. I promised you that a long time ago. So, yeah. I hired a gun: the best, I was told. Trouble is, you got the Devil's luck while I get the dirty end of the stick.'

'I never counted busted ribs as lucky,' said Jubal, anger flattening his voice to a rasp. 'What happened to Andy?'

'Jesus, I don't know!' Agnew's wail was genuinely anguished. 'Klein took my money an' the boy too.'

'Get up,' said Jubal. 'You got a whole lot of talking to do. May as well do it from a chair.'

Still holding the Colt on the sweating businessman, he reached for the whiskey glass, passing it across. Then he filled a second and settled himself into the facing chair.

'Who's Klein?'

'A hired gun.' Agnew sounded resigned, as though he had lost all hope. 'I paid him five thousand dollars to kill you. He said he'd done it.'

'He got close,' said Jubal, swallowing whiskey to kill the pain in his ribs. 'What about Andy?'

'Oh Christ!' Agnew's discomfort was unfaked. 'The bastard took my money, then took the boy. He wants fifteen thousand to send him back.'

'From where?' Jubal asked.

'Some one-horse town called Angel. It's in Kansas.'

'You paid him yet?'

'No.' Agnew bowed his head, rubbing at an unshaven cheek. 'I sent word that I would. Now I'm waiting to hear from him.'

'How about the Pinkerton you hired?' Jubal curbed his impatience, recognizing the need to gather as much information as he could. 'What's he turned up?'

'Nothing yet,' muttered Agnew. 'He's not been gone more'n a week. Took the train out to Angel. I'm waiting on both of them.'

Jubal nodded, assimilating information. 'What's Klein look like?'

'An albino. White hair, pale skin, red eyes. Dresses all in black.' Agnew hunted his memory for fresh recollections. 'Talks soft. Northern accent. I heard he came from Salt Lake City originally. Uses a Smith & Wesson Russian. That much I noticed; no more.'

'Shouldn't be hard to spot,' grunted Jubal.

'But hard to stop,' said Agnew. 'He's a killer, a real hard-case.'

'You should know,' grated Jubal. 'You hired him.'

'Oh God! I wish I hadn't.' Agnew sounded genuinely regretful. 'If I'd known it would come to this I'd have called off the deal.'

'As Andy would say,' murmured Jubal, 'there's no use crying over spilled milk. Nor blood, for that matter. You said the place was called Angel? In Kansas?'

Agnew nodded. 'Yeah. Why?'

'Because I'm going there,' answered the grubby, hurting figure. 'To find Andy.'

Agnew looked up, drawing his hands down his stubbly face. His eyes were bloodshot, the pouchy cheeks sucked in so that he looked suddenly much older than his natural years. For a moment something like hope shone through the worry, and he almost smiled.

'You might just bring it off, Cade.'

He said it like an afterthought, rising ponderously from his chair to fumble in the desk. He found what he was looking for, and crossed to the safe. Opening the metal cabinet, he reached inside, hauling out a wad of bills. Then he crossed the carpet to stand in front of Jubal, holding out the money.

'There's five thousand. Take it. I promised Gloria that I'd look out for Andy, an' if you're the only hope I got, then I guess I have to stake you.'

Jubal looked up, surprised. Agnew seemed genuine. It was a tempting offer: five thousand could leave enough over after travel expenses to pay for Andy's operation. The trouble was taking it from the man who had tried to kill him. Then his ribs hurt again, a sudden twinge lancing pain through his side, and he remembered that Agnew *had* tried to kill him, on more than one occasion.* And he reached out to take the wad of notes.

'All right. I'll take it to cover the trip. It doesn't change anything though. You better understand that, Agnew. So long as Andy wants to stick with me, I stay his legal guardian. If I find Klein and get Andy back, he goes straight into the clinic again. Under my care.'

Agnew nodded, and for a moment Jubal felt sympathy for the man. He had money – more than Jubal was ever likely to see – and power, land, possessions. But he lacked the important thing: respect sided by love. All he had instead was money.

'If you hear anything send a wire to Angel.' He rose as he said it, wincing at the pain in his side. 'I'll collect messages from the telegraph depot.'

He rode down to the St. Louis terminal and booked passage on the next train west for himself and the bay horse. The ticket clerk gave a doubting look at his worn clothes, but the billfold convinced him and he passed out the long roll of interstop coupons without further delay.

Jubal glanced at the wad of money, amused by the situation of its donation, then he shrugged, settling down to wait for the incoming train.

'I suppose,' he murmured to himself, 'that you'd call it robbing Agnew to pay for Andy.'

* See: Jubal Cade – *Vengeance Hunt*.

CHAPTER FIVE

The locomotive was a big, brassy Baldwin 4-4-0. Someone had put a great deal of effort into polishing the cowcatcher and sidelights, and even the bulk of the boiler cylinder looked to be washed down. Starchy miniatures of Old Glory fluttered to either side of the high-riding smokestack, and as she came out of the engine sheds Jubal wondered if he was riding a presidential train again. He hoped not: the last time had been too dangerous.*

The loco wheezed along past the platform, shrilling to a halt with three Pullman cars dropping footrails down to the planking. Jubal headed for the nearest car. He was reaching for the handrail when a pair of elaborately tooled boots stepped into view and a harsh voice cut through the darkness.

'Not this one, friend. She's reserved.'

Jubal looked up into a cold, grey stare emphasized by the negligent droop of a twin-muzzle Remington scattergun. So negligent the big dark holes were pointed straight at his chest.

Jubal backed off. A man didn't argue with a scattergun.

'Henry! What's the trouble?' The second voice was deep and mellow, a soothing tone with undercurrents of command.

The man with the shotgun glanced back inside the car, still holding the Remington on Jubal. 'Nothing, Senator. Some passenger mistook his place.' He turned back to look down at the platform, nodding over his shoulder. 'Senator Brady's got these two reserved, friend. You get the front car.'

Jubal shrugged and set out up the platform. It explained the brasswork and the flags. It might also make for a faster journey: the KP would pull out the stops with a US Senator travelling on board. He reached the forward Pullman and climbed inside. The car was mostly empty and he picked a

* See: Jubal Cade – *Death Wears Grey*.

46

seat in the middle, stowing his saddle under the bench. Then he stretched out across the seat and went to sleep. He woke up in Kansas City with the sun on his face and a grinning porter watching him.

'I clipped yore tickets so far, mister, but I hafta tell you: I ain't never seen a man sleep through so much excitement.'

Jubal sat up, holding his ribs against the pain of movement. 'What excitement? What's been happening?'

'Man!' The porter kept on smiling. 'You don't know what train you're ridin'? You ain't heard o' Senator Brady?'

Jubal shook his head, wondering where he could find a washroom.

'No. Who is he?'

'You, sir,' the porter stood up dramatically, 'are on the Brady Flier. The Senator is headin' through to his home town. Angel, Kansas, that is. The fair new settlement that has just won its right to call itself a town. Up till now Angel weren't no more'n a few shacks an' a water tank. It is now a *town*. Officially. An' the Senator is headin' back to cut the ribbon on progress an' prosperity.' He leaned closer, confidential. 'It also has a remarkable fine cathouse. A man wishin' an introduction would be advised to take the word of a benevolent friend.'

Jubal understood his meaning and grinned, shaking his head. 'No thanks. The last time I got mixed up with a bunch of whores I near lost a good watch; and a few other things besides.'*

The porter shrugged, his gesture eloquently suggesting that Jubal was missing more than he knew. He pointed the way to the washroom and, in return for a quarter, agreed to bring hot water and towels. Jubal followed his directions, finding the small cubicle empty. He stripped down to the waist and sluiced his upper body with cold water from the jug. When the man brought a steaming kettle of water fresh-drawn from the engine, he stripped down to the buff and bathed his wounds. Painfully, he rewound the bandages, then

* See: Jubal Cade – *The Hungry Gun.*

47

shaved. He was still hurting, but freshening up made him feel better, and the journey west should give him time enough to heal up. At least enough for his purpose.

The Brady Flier pulled out of Kansas City on a line running midway between the Saline and the Smoky Hill rivers. It went on past Topeka and a drab little place called Abilene that stank of cows, a second, indistinguishable township called Ellsworth, and then across the open plain. Jubal lost count of the days, though he knew they passed faster than they would on horseback. And finally, they reached Angel.

It was close on sunset, the long quiet that preceded nightfall seeming to still the lonely Kansas plains with a lazy silence that was broken only by the shrieking of the locomotive's whistle. The ear-splitting sound woke Jubal from a light sleep, and he stuck his head out of the window, peering towards the Flier's destination.

At first glance, Angel looked like nowhere. So far as he could tell, there were only three buildings reaching over two storeys, and most were single-floor places. Apart from a blaze of light around the rail depot, the town was dark, and Jubal wondered how hard a Senator had to work to retain his home-town vote. He had seen nothing of Brady throughout the journey. The rear two Pullmans were locked off from the other, the door in from the observation platform permanently shut. According to the porter, the Senator brought special staff with him, cooks, waiters and valets included alongside the shotgun-carrying bodyguards. He had boarded the train early, back in St. Louis, and remained aloof within his personal cars ever since. He was planning to spend no more than two days in Angel; after that, his Pullmans would be coupled onto the first eastbound train and towed back to St. Louis, the Senator's duty done and the town forgotten until the next civic occasion demanded his presence.

Jubal grinned cynically, leaning back with his feet up, waiting for the locomotive to grind to a halt.

As they pulled in to the whistlestop station, he saw bunting strung across the street, welcoming Angel's very own

48

home-grown Senator. The bright Kansas sun had bleached the canvas so that the paint was faded down, hard to make out. Less so, the people waiting to greet Brady. There was a big crowd gathered around the depot, and when the echoes of the whistle faded away, Jubal caught the raucous blare of a small band.

The locomotive shuddered into final rest and a swell of local dignitaries surged around the rearward Pullmans. Brady's bodyguards climbed down first, shouldering an avenue through the crowd, and Jubal saw the Senator. He was a tall, white-haired man, dressed in a light grey coat with a dark blue vest that accentuated the impeccable whiteness of his shirt. The brilliance of the linen was matched by the flash of his teeth as he gifted the cheering crowd with a professional smile. Jubal watched the stately figure disappear into the ticket office followed by his retinue, and rose from his seat. The few other passengers had already hurried out to join in the celebrations, and he climbed down onto a near-empty platform. At the rear of the train, the box-car was open and two sweating railhands were hauling a ramp up to the sliding doors. Jubal walked inside, taking the bay horse's halter to lead it out. He got the animal down to the ground and slung his saddle loose over the sturdy back, then walked the beast off in search of a hotel.

At close quarters, Angel was as unprepossessing as it had looked from out on the plain. Two of the tall buildings were hotels, one belonged to the local Cattleman's Association, the third was empty and up for sale.

He checked into the smaller of the two rooming houses and arranged stabling for the horse. Then he went to find the telegraph office.

It was located in a small, single-storey building halfway down Angel's solitary street, and the door was locked. Jubal had to wait until Senator Brady was settled safely into the larger of the two hotels before the telegraph clerk returned, flushed with excitement, to re-open the place.

'Name's Cade.' Jubal's ribs were hurting too much to waste

49

time being polite. 'You got any messages for me?'

The clerk rummaged through the pigeonholes behind his desk and shook his head. 'Nossir. Ain't nothin' fer anyone o' that name.'

Jubal reached into his vest, pulling out a silver dollar. 'Anything from a man called Agnew?'

'Sir!' The clerk sounded affronted. But he didn't take his eyes off the coin. 'That'd be breakin' company rules.'

Jubal let the coin fall onto the counter. It disappeared fast. 'Were a couple o' wires, now I come to think.'

The clerk paused, eyeing Jubal speculatively. A second coin loosened his tongue. 'Was one more'n two weeks back. Reply to Mr. Klein's message. Somethin' about money.'

Jubal held his patience in check with difficulty, not wishing to reveal his interest too obviously. 'Mr. Klein collect it?'

'Why, sure.' The clerk was warming to the conversation, sensing a topic of interesting gossip. 'Come right in the next mornin' to collect it.'

'He still around?' Jubal tried to make it sound like he was enquiring after a friend. 'Agnew gave me a message for him.'

'Don't rightly know,' said the clerk. 'I don't recall seein' him lately. They'd know down at the Kansas Palace. He was stayin' there.'

Jubal nodded thoughtfully and turned to go. Then halted when the clerk called after him.

'Was two wires, I said.' Jubal turned, listening. But the man smiled, one hand splayed out palm-upwards on the counter. 'The other should be worth a dollar more.'

Jubal tossed the coin over.

'Come in a few days ago. Addressed to Elias Holden at the Palace. Said to watch out fer Jubal Cade arrivin'. Reckon that one referred to you.'

Jubal watched the man for a moment, his eyes cold. Then he grinned and opened the door. Halfway through he paused, looking back.

'You ever hear the one about the clerk who listened at keyholes?'

'Nope.' The man shook his head, anticipating a dirty story. 'Cain't say I have.'

'Someone opened the door,' murmured Jubal. 'Stuck the handle clear through the man's skull. It killed him stone dead.'

He walked away, ignoring the spluttering from inside the office.

He was booked into the Prairie Garden Hotel; the Kansas Palace was on the opposite side of the dirt street, several buildings farther up. It was the one he made for. Inside, it resembled most mid-western hotels: shabby grandeur fighting hard to look respectable under a layer of prairie dust and the attacks of cowmen's spurs. Wilting cacti plants stood in for the aspidistras of the East, and the brocade chairs looked to have been shipped out on the earliest wagon train. A central chandelier was in bad need of cleaning, and the brightest point in the vestibule was the banner strung from one side to the other, announcing: ANGEL WELCOMES HER NATIVE SON. LONG LIVE IVES BRADY.

From the noise coming out of the dining-room, Jubal guessed that most of Angel was busy doing just that. He crossed to the reception desk and punched the bell. The tinny rattle brought a sleek-haired receptionist scurrying to the source of the interruption. He eyed Jubal's clothes, decided he couldn't be with the Senator's party, and began to speak before he got behind the desk.

'Sorry. We're full.'

'That must be a change for you,' said Jubal, laconically. 'Still, being full should clear the dust some.'

The man ran a hand over his brilliantined hair, not sure what to make of this new visitor. Something in Jubal's face persuaded him to forget the rudeness and try tact instead.

'I'm sorry, sir. But the Senator's party has taken every room.'

'Even Klein's?' Jubal asked innocently.

'Mr. Klein?' The man looked nervous and surprised at the same time. It was a combination that distorted his lugubrious

51

features into a resemblance to a sick spaniel. 'You know him?'

Jubal nodded. 'I got an appointment with him.'

More or less it was the truth.

'I'm sorry, sir. Mr. Klein checked out several days ago.'

'You sure?' Jubal asked. 'You got the right Klein? Tall man, very pale. Wears black.'

The clerk chuckled, smoothing a strand of wispy hair over his skull. 'You must be mistaken. Mr. Klein is dark, and he wore a brown suit during his stay.'

Jubal registered surprise. Agnew might have lied about Klein's appearance, but it seemed unlikely. Andy had been kidnapped and the rancher's grief had appeared genuine. There was no reason for him to lie – unless he was setting Jubal up for a second ambush.

'How about a man called Holden?' He asked. 'Elias Holden?'

Again the clerk shook his head, growing bored. 'No. Never had anyone of that name in. I'm sorry, but I can't help. And now I really must get back.'

He ducked his head, showing Jubal a grease-smeared patch of hairless skin, and hurried around the desk, anxious to return to the festivities. Jubal watched him go, a quizzical expression twisting his mouth. If Agnew had been telling the truth, then Klein had to be working with an accomplice. Holden might have checked in under a false name, in which case he would have to rely on Agnew's description to locate the Pinkerton. Unless the telegraph clerk could provide one.

He went back to the office.

'What you want now?' The clerk was less friendly.

'Klein,' said Jubal, 'what did he look like?'

'Like I forget,' grunted the clerk. 'What the hell you think I am, some kind o' information service?'

'No,' said Jubal, crossing the small office in two long strides.

The clerk backed off as he saw the expression on Jubal's face. The unassuming little guy who had handed out dollars for gossip earlier in the day was gone. In his place stood a dangerous man. Anger had got the better of Jubal and his eyes blazed with barely controlled rage, his lips thinning out as the skin across his cheek-bones stretched taut, the scar tissue crossing the bridge of his nose standing out white against his tan. The clerk failed to move fast enough, because Jubal's outstretched hand caught him before he could reach the door leading to his rear office. It hooked around his shirtfront, tugging the cheap cloth loose from the waistband of his pants as he was yanked forwards over the counter.

Emile Bennet had operated the Angel telegraph office for three years. During that time he had seen the bank robbed twice, and once been held at gunpoint himself while three outlaws waited for a US marshal to come in after them. Emile had been frightened on each occasion. Now, he was terrified. He could feel the rough edge of the desk rasping against his groin, and the grip on his shirt was threatening to choke him. Worst of all, though, were the eyes boring into his. He remembered them as brown, and rather soft; now they blazed, like two coals burning in a hot fire. Hot enough to make him sweat despite the breeze blowing off the prairie.

'Klein,' grated Jubal. 'What does he look like?'

'Short,' gasped Emile, finding it hard to speak, 'around your size. Dark hair. Wore it long. Had a Texas accent, an' he wore a brown suit.'

'The other man.' Jubal dragged down on Emile's shirt, pressing his throat against the counter. 'Holden. Describe him.'

'Tall.' Emile spluttered, fighting for breath. 'Older, judgin' from the grey in his hair. Looked tired. Jesus! You're chokin' me to death.'

'You shouldn't talk so much,' grated Jubal, and let the man go.

Emile slid backwards off the desk, falling to the floor with both hands massaging his bruised throat. After a while, he stood up and risked looking across the office. The man was gone. Emile hoped he wouldn't come back.

Jubal didn't intend to. He believed that he had as much information from the telegraph clerk as he could hope for, though it didn't help him any. So far all he knew was that Klein – and Andy with him – were not around Angel; a stooge, or a partner, must have sent the message to Agnew and collected the reply. Holden was another problem. The Pinkerton was obviously using a false name, which left Jubal only his description to go on. If he was still around Angel, it shouldn't be hard to find him. If he was gone, it would be near impossible. Jubal hoped he was still around, because he wanted to find Saul Klein on his own. It was partly a matter of personal pride linked with a desire for vengeance; mostly it was because he felt he had a better chance of getting Andy back safe than any professional detective.

He glanced down Angel's lonely mainstreet. No one should be hard to find here.

To his right was a hardware store and a grainery, behind him, the telegraph office. Beyond that stood a milliners, a second hardware store, a bank, a saloon, and the Prairie Garden Hotel. Siding that was the tall façade of the Cattleman's Association, an eating house and a general store. Then the street ended in Kansas dust. The far side of the street boasted the Kansas Palace, the sheriff's office, a stage station, a livery stable, and a scattering of small stores selling anything from barbed wire to ribbons.

Thoughtfully, he lit a cheroot, inhaling the aromatic smoke deep into his lungs. No one should be hard to find here. Unless they were being hidden.

He went back to his hotel and ordered dinner. The service was good because most people had swapped to the Kansas Palace in order to get a chance to see the Senator, leaving Jubal alone with an elderly itinerant preacher and two maiden ladies awaiting the next train through to St. Louis. After casting a disapproving glance at his clothes, they all settled back to their meals, deciding that the shabby little man with the stiff arm was not worth speaking to. Jubal was grateful for the silence, just as he was grateful for the extra-large portions. His wounds were hurting again, and what he wanted more than anything was a good meal and a night's solid sleep in a soft bed. The hurt died down to a dull ache, but every so often a lance of pain burned its way up his side and he was forced to remember Lenz's comment about not letting a patient up with wounds of that kind. He had to agree. The steak and fries, however, went a long way to offsetting the discomfort, and by the time he had worked his way through a second helping, agreed to a double portion of blueberry pie, and swallowed half a pot of coffee, he felt a whole lot better and ready to sleep.

His room was situated on the second floor, facing out over mainstreet. And he was glad to enter it: the bed looked very comfortable. It was, and he fell asleep within minutes, easing his body over the ache in his side.

Something disturbed his sleep and he moved restlessly, shifting over in the soft bed. The disturbance came again and he woke up, turning to cover the opening of his eyes. Surreptitiously, he burrowed one hand under the pillow, hunting the butt of the Colt.

He found it, his fingers clasping around the smooth wood grip. The gun slid out from the pillow with the hammer shifting back and the muzzle lining on the man beside his bed. Then the heavy bore of a .44 Remington shone through the darkness like a black beacon, and he slumped back, though the Colt stayed pointed at the intruder.

'Take it easy, Cade.' The voice was low and husky, almost friendly. 'I only want to talk to you.'

'In the middle of the night?' Jubal was doubtful. 'Who the hell are you?'

'Name's Holden.' The voice sounded like the speaker expected Jubal to recognize the name. 'I work for the Pinkerton Agency. Ben Agnew hired me to find Andy ...'

'Prescott.' Jubal interrupted. 'I know. Agnew told me about you. I came looking for Andy too.'

'Don't,' said Holden. 'You won't find him. I spent the last week here, and he ain't around.'

'Holden,' answered Jubal, 'you shouldn't tell me to forget the boy. If you can't find him, I will.'

Jubal could just make out the smile on Holden's face in the gloom. He didn't like it.

'Like I said, Cade: forget it. I got a fat reward riding on this case. I don't want amateurs muscling in.'

'Why not, Holden?' Jubal was unpleasantly aware of the gun muzzle pointed at his forehead. 'You afraid I might lose you that reward?'

'Something like that,' grunted Holden. 'Apart from which, amateurs tend to screw things up.'

'Sorry,' Jubal said slowly, 'but I got a personal stake. I'm looking for the boy. If we can work together, fine. If not, you go your way, me mine. Don't try to stop me either way.'

Holden smiled, bringing the Remington closer to Jubal's face. The cold metal of the barrel pressed his forehead, the knuckle of the Pinkerton's trigger finger huge in the distorted perspective. Instinctively, Jubal levelled his gun on the man's belly.

'Seems to me like we got a Mexican stand-off,' he said quietly. 'You fire and you're dead.'

'They said you were tricky,' agreed Holden. 'I guess it takes the findin' to know.'

'Try anything and you'll learn the certainty,' agreed Jubal. 'Otherwise, back off and get out. We can talk in the morning.'

Holden nodded cautiously, abruptly aware that he was up against a man he couldn't frighten. Slowly, taking care not to make any sudden moves, he lowered the hammer of the Remington. He slid the revolver back into its holster and moved for the door. Jubal kept the Colt levelled at the Pinkerton's stomach.

'Breakfast?' Holden's voice was unsure. 'Here?'

'Why not?' Jubal nodded his assent. 'One thing though.'

'What?' The Pinkerton stopped with the door half-open.

'Don't pull a gun on me again,' said Jubal. 'Next time I'll kill you.'

Holden nodded and slid quietly through the door. He made

noise going down the corridor, and Jubal waited until it was gone before he climbed out of bed to relock the picked door and jam a chair under the handle. Then he went back to sleep. In the morning he took his time shaving, and enjoyed a long, hot bath before heading down to the dining-room. Holden was already there, sipping coffee in a nervous kind of way while he waited. Jubal joined him.

There was a tenseness between them, but the duel of wills the previous night seemed to have fixed some kind of ground rules and Holden was more respectful now that Jubal had bested him.

'Maybe we should compare notes,' he said reluctantly.

'Go ahead,' murmured Jubal, ' or shall we flip a coin to decide who starts?'

Holden grinned and shook his head, beginning to talk.

He knew about as much as Jubal. A short, dark man had posed as Klein, sending the first wire and collecting the answer. After that he had disappeared. He rode a piebald gelding and, when last seen, was heading southwest. That had been a day before Holden arrived. The Pinkerton had opted to stay around Angel because it was his only contact point with Agnew: if Klein sent another message, the rancher could relay it to the detective in Angel; otherwise, he would be gone with no real lead to follow. The absence of news tied him to the little Kansas town as surely as a rope.

'One thing I learned though,' he grunted, pouring fresh coffee for them both. 'Klein is known in these parts. Used to run with a jayhawker outfit from around the Arkansas. Seems there's a saddle of hills to the southwest where they had a hide-out. A place called Deadman Crossing. River cuts through the rock, and the cliffs are full of caves. Klein used to lead his men outta there.'

'You checked it?' Jubal asked.

'No.' Holden shook his head, shrugging. 'How could I? It's three days' ride away an' there's no sure guarantee Klein's there. I want to stick someplace close to the telegraph in case Agnew sends fresh word.'

Jubal thought for a moment, weighing the alternatives. Holden had the backing of the Pinkerton Detective Agency with all its resources and its money; he, Jubal, was a man alone. Teaming up with Holden might – just – be a wise move.

'Suppose,' he said slowly, 'that I rode out to Deadman Crossing? You hang on here; I can come back with any news. If I don't, you know it's bad.'

Holden looked thoughtful. 'What about the money?'

'Agnew gave me five thousand,' said Jubal, choosing to lay his cards on the table. 'It's enough for me. There's a reward out from the Lenz Clinic for five hundred dollars, plus whatever Klein fetches. You can take all of that if we get Andy back.'

Holden stared into his cup, his eyes blinking as he thought about it.

'You mean you'd turn down the whole reward? Why?'

'Andy means a lot to me,' said Jubal evenly. 'I want him safe. The money's nothing.'

'You know, Cade,' said Holden slowly, 'I believe you. I'm willing to try it your way.'

'All right,' nodded Jubal, 'come morning, I'll make for the hills. You stick around here. If anything comes through on the wire, you can ride out to find me.'

Holden ducked his head in agreement, extending a hand across the table. They shook.

'Just remember, Cade,' he said, 'that the Pinkerton Agency is the eye that never sleeps. I take the money.'

'Like a vote, isn't it?' Jubal grinned. 'The ayes get it.'

CHAPTER SIX

Angel threw a hoedown in the Senator's honour that evening. Lanterns were strung across mainstreet, their yellow glow casting shadows over the trestle tables piled with food. Heavy beer kegs were manhandled out of the saloon and mounted on sawhorses along the boardwalk, and a punch bowl prepared for the ladies. Both ends of the street were roped off while a team of volunteers set to raking the dust clear of horse apples in readiness for the dancing. A wagon was dragged over to the front of the Kansas Palace and draped with the Stars and Stripes and the Kansas state flag: it was to serve as a rostrum for Brady's speech. Throughout the day, the town entertained a festive air. The saloon did a roaring trade in hard liquor as cowboys from the outlying ranches and groups of farmers drifted in.

Jubal watched it happening from the shade of the verandah outside the Prairie Garden, Holden seated beside him, feet hiked up on the hitching rail. There had been no word from Agnew and Jubal was contemplating riding out straight away. Common sense, however, prompted him to wait: it could be a hard ride, and a day of rest might well make a big difference. His ribs were knitting cleanly, and the powder burns along his side were mostly healed over. The holes in his chest and shoulder, though, were slower to heal. His left arm remained stiff, and every so often the wound over his ribs twinged painfully. On balance he decided that one more day wouldn't make too much difference. Except to his temper. If Klein planned to get in touch with Agnew again, the chances were he would send the message from the town. The only other telegraph office in five days' ride was located at Nixon, a much larger settlement. Jubal doubted the kidnapper would risk showing himself there, or that his mysterious accomplice

59

would take the chance: Nixon had a mean reputation for shooting first and worrying about the legalities afterwards. So he opted to wait.

'Looks to be some wing-ding.' Holden gestured at the activity in the street.

'Yeah,' said Jubal absently.

'You're blockin' the sidewalk.' The voice was harsh, vaguely familiar. 'Whyn't you go loaf someplace else?'

Jubal turned, looking up at the speaker. It was the shotgun-toting guard from the Brady Flier, still carrying the ugly Remington and still looking mean.

'Hi, Henry.' Jubal remembered the man's name. 'You can always walk around us.'

'Or over you,' rasped Henry. 'You gonna move, or not?'

He hefted the scattergun as he spoke, fixing his cold stare on Jubal's face. Obviously he rated the smaller man low on his list of people to worry about.

Jubal grinned lazily. 'Guess not,' he murmured. 'It's kind of comfortable here.'

Henry was on the point of saying something else when a deep, smooth-toned voice butted in.

'Henry!' For all its smoothness, the voice held undertones of iron. 'What's the trouble?'

'Nuthin', Senator,' muttered Henry, reluctantly. 'Just askin' these folks to move outta the way.'

'No need,' smiled the politician. 'We're here to meet people, not move them. Gentlemen.' He moved past his bodyguard, smiling as he held out his right hand. 'I'm Ives Brady. Born and raised in Angel, and still glad to be back home. Who're you?'

'Jubal Cade,' said Jubal, shaking the politician's hand.

'Holden,' said the Pinkerton. 'Elias Holden.'

'Glad to know you.' Brady pumped the handshake with professional enthusiasm. 'You from around here?'

'No,' Jubal answered. 'We're just passing through.'

'That so?' Brady was appraising them as he spoke, checking over their clothes. 'On business?'

'Well,' grinned Jubal, 'I don't imagine too many people visit Angel for pleasure.'

Brady smiled, nodding, although he obviously found it hard to maintain the diplomatic bonhomie in the face of Jubal's cynicism.

'Guess not, though it's a great little town. Got a big future. Well, I'll be seeing you, gentlemen.'

Jubal and Holden sat down again as the Senator moved on past them, flanked by Henry and another bodyguard.

Jubal watched them go. 'Wonder why he needs the guns around?'

'You ain't heard?' Holden looked surprised.

Jubal shook his head.

'Ives Brady's a big man in the Senate right now.' The Pinkerton drew his chair in closer, as though wary of being overheard. 'Highly regarded by the right people. Especially the ones with well-greased palms. He showed up a year or so after the War, carpetbaggin' his way around with a whole lot o' money. Considerin' his folks come from here when Angel weren't no more than a way-station an' a water-hole, an' never had more than they needed to buy the next bag o' flour, it was a might too easy to be honest.'

The detective stared after the retreating figure of the Senator. Brady had reached the end of the street and was crossing over to the far side, continuing his round of handshaking and casual chatter. Holden directed a gobbet of chewing tobacco at the street.

'There's no record of him having served with either side during the war. Course, that don't necessarily mean anythin': lot o' the records got lost one way or another. He claims to have been in the Union cavalry an' wounded at Glorietta. There ain't no way to prove it. Or argue it, come to that. Me, I reckon he was a Kansas jayhawker, an' his money come out of loot.'

Jubal was intrigued. 'How come you know so much about him?'

'Business,' said Holden succinctly. 'The Agency keeps a

file on most important people. A few years back, we was asked to check Brady out. I remembered the details when I heard I was headin' for Angel.'

He shrugged and lapsed into silence, cutting a fresh hunk of tobacco from his wad. Jubal lit a cheroot, and both men settled back to watch the citizens prepare for the hoedown.

It began at sunset. Angel looked a better town at that time of day, with the huge red-gold orb of the sun going down way out across the prairie. The wind-scoured frontages of the buildings were bathed in a soft, golden light that hid the peeling paint and threw long, soft shadows over the cracked boards and fly-specked glass of the store fronts. The lanterns hung over mainstreet were lit and the little town was suddenly gaudy, preening itself as it waited to become – officially – a registered township.

Ives Brady came out of the Kansas Palace with a big smile on his face and a fresh-pressed white suit flattering his tan. He lifted both arms in greeting to the crowd cheering him from the street, and climbed onto the decorated wagon. The two bodyguards clambered up beside him. The civic dignitaries followed, all three of them.

The Senator began his speech with a flourish: 'Citizens of Angel. Yes! Citizens, now that Angel is – officially – a town.' There was a cheer from the crowd. 'I am pleased to be back here. Here in my home town. It makes a man feel proud to come home and find the place where he was born flourishing, growing into a rich and thriving community that ...'

'Bullshit,' grunted Holden. 'You want a drink?'

'... A community that shines like a bright jewel on the fair face of Kansas. A spreading centre of ...'

'Beats listening,' replied Jubal. 'Let's go.'

'... And promises to grow still larger,' intoned Brady, 'exerting its influence far and wide over the plains and prairies of our native land. A place of ...'

Jubal followed the Pinkerton into the saloon. The Laughing Lady was emptier than it had been all day. Most of the drinkers were outside, listening goggle-eyed to the oration.

'... But greater things are yet to come.' Brady's voice carried in through the batwing doors. 'The time when Angel will have a church, a school. When street lights will line the spreading sidewalks, and stone replace the dust of mainstreet. A time when ...'

'Goes on some, don't he?' Holden grunted, ordering whiskey. 'Guess he's anxious for the vote.'

'Sounds that way,' grinned Jubal. 'How long you think he'll keep talking?'

Holden shrugged, aiming a jet of tobacco juice at a handy spittoon.

'... From the dust of the Kansas plains she will rise, a growing, glowing gem. A proud town, a fine city ...'

The shot interrupted the speech as abruptly as cold water poured over a howling cat. It crackled through the still air, punctuating Brady's sentence with a dramatic finality. For long moments there was utter silence. Then shouting broke out along with the crisp barking of rifles.

Sided by Holden, Jubal ran for the doors. People were screaming outside, milling around the street in panic as the hidden marksmen cut them down like scared chickens. Jubal stayed under the verandah, keeping close to the wall of the saloon with the Pinkerton behind him. The Colt was in his hand, hammer back on a tight trigger; but he could see no target. From over his shoulder Holden shouted.

'What the hell's goin' on?'

'I don't know.' Jubal dropped to a crouch, looking up at the roofs of the surrounding buildings, trying to spot the gun-flashes.

The chaos in the street caught his attention, and he dropped his gaze in time to see a woman spin around, her poke bonnet flying from her head as a slug lifted away the upper section of her face. She pirouetted a neat circle, trailing blood-spattered skirts through the dust, then doubled over, crushing the stained bonnet beneath her corpse. Close by, a man dropped the mug he was holding, spilling beer in a frothy circle, and ran towards her. A bullet caught him in the leg, pitching him

63

face-down. He pushed up, rising to his feet again, and began to limp towards the body of the fallen woman. A second bullet hit his shoulder, slamming him sideways without knocking him down. He ignored it, staggering onwards with blood gouting from the two wounds. A third punctured his stomach. It entered above his waist, exiting in a spray of blood and flesh from his back, and he twisted over like a closed jackknife.

Ives Brady moved off the wagon with maximum speed and minimum dignity. The civic officer immediately to his right was falling sideways with a gaping hole through his throat as the Senator hurled himself under cover of the verandah. His two bodyguards loosed all four barrels of their scatterguns at nothing in particular and followed him.

On the street, five bodies stretched, bleeding.

'The empty building!' Holden shouted into Jubal's ear. 'Two men.'

'I see them.' Jubal looked towards the empty windows, catching the blast of fast-fired rifles. 'Must be more above us though.'

Holden nodded. 'Want to try for them?'

'Sure,' rasped Jubal.

They went back into the Laughing Lady. The saloon was a double-storey place with a narrow stairwell rising up to the second floor. A balcony overlooked the room below, with doors opening off it into the sleeping quarters. Holden led the way, running past the deserted bedrooms to a vertical ladder that disappeared up into the roof. He climbed the thing, pushing against a trapdoor at the top. Opened, it led out to the flat roof. Holden went through fast, then ducked his head back in to motion Jubal to follow.

The roof of the saloon was covered with tar paper tacked onto solid planking, its forward end overshadowed by a false frontage that lifted ten feet higher than the real roof. It afforded the cover they needed.

The deserted building was directly opposite, and Jubal could see two men firing rifles from inside the empty rooms.

64

They were out of range of the pistol, so he turned, seeking a closer target. The neighbouring building was a single-storey grocery, built at a slight angle to the street so that its low roof commanded a wide angle of fire. Two men stretched there, rifles aimed down into the crowd.

'I'll take the right,' whispered Jubal. 'You get the guy on the left.'

Holden nodded, clasping both hands around the butt of the Remington.

Jubal levelled the Peacemaker on the man's back, bracing his extended arm against the gun's kick. He sighted carefully, and squeezed the trigger.

The .45 calibre slug hit the sniper between the shoulder-blades. It broke his spine on impact, jerking his body up and over like a dying fish. The rifle flew from his opened hands, tumbling down into the street as its owner fell forwards, his arms spread wide. Holden's man died with two bullets in his chest and blood on his face. Then more rifles opened up from the other buildings, and this time around, their fire was directed at the men on the roof.

'It's getting unhealthy up here,' Jubal shouted over the noise. 'Let's try it from downstairs.'

'Yeah.' The Pinkerton ducked under a fusillade that blew splinters from the frontage of the saloon. 'I think you're right.'

They went back down the ladder and out to the doors. The street was still jammed with people, most of them cowering behind whatever cover they could find. Children were scream-ing louder than their mothers, and a group of cowboys was blasting wildly at roofs and windows, without hitting anything except glass and tarpaulin. Ives Brady was crouched inside the Kansas Palace, his bodyguards riding shotgun on the door. Then, from the decorated wagon, came a commanding bellow.

'Hold it! Hold it!' The firing eased. 'It's the sheriff speakin'. Now quit this.'

The silence was very loud. Then, out into the glow of the lamps came a portly figure. The belt that supported his trousers was mostly hidden beneath the spread of his belly, and the gun hung on his right hip looked to be obscured by the rolls of fat. But gross though he was, he did not lack courage. Lifting both hands into clear view, he walked out to the centre of the street.

'Crazy,' murmured Jubal, looking up at the rifle-sprouting windows.

'You know me. Vance Graves.' The sheriff was in his mid-forties. 'Been the law here fer nine years now. I don't know what this's all about, but I do know fer sure there ain't no cause to it.'

Jubal couldn't make up his mind whether the man was a hero, or a fool. Maybe both.

'Bin folks killed,' shouted Graves. 'Enuff to stir up more fuss than makes it worth while. Whatever the reason. Now I'm tellin' you to leave it off afore it goes too far.'

'Too far?' A woman screamed from the shadows. 'That's my husband out there. He's dead. That's too far already.'

Graves waved his hands in a vaguely placatory motion, looking nervously around.

'I know, ma'am. But what's done stays done. Ain't no use to weepin' over it.'

'Well said, Vance.' The new voice was soft, bitter with cynical amusement, and it stopped the sheriff in mid-sentence. 'But you always did have a way with words.'

From out of the shadows came the slow *clopping* of hooves as a big black stallion walked slowly forwards into the light. The rider was dressed all in black, pants, coat, vest, and even his shirt, combining to offset the stark paleness of his hair and skin. The lanterns threw shafts of light against his bright red eyes, so that he looked more like some demon ridden in to claim souls than a human man.

But Jubal recognized Saul Klein from Agnew's description.

'In case anyone's thinkin' of shooting me,' called the albino, 'they better think twice. There's men on the roofs an' more up the street.' His words were backed by a stealthy movement of armed men from both ends of Angel. 'Ain't no reason

66

for anyone else to get hurt, not now that you know we can kill you stone dead where you stand.'

Jubal checked the riders. There were too many to make a fight worth while, and he dropped his gun gently back into the holster.

'Someone tried a fight, Saul.' The shout came from the empty building. 'Was someone shot Zeke an' Ike.'

'Who?' Klein's voice cracked like a whiplash. 'Who did it?'

There was a long silence, marred by the shuffling of frightened feet and the whimpering of children.

'You have to learn.' Klein's voice carried the same way the Senator's had. 'I'll count to five. After that we open fire. Unless you give me the man who did it.'

The silence went on for a long time.

'One.'

'Oh, God, he means it,' cried a woman.

'Two.'

'You gonna kill a whole town?' shouted a cowboy.

'Three.'

'He will,' said Graves into the nervous quiet. 'He will.'

'Four.'

'Sweet Christ, I don't want to die. Please don't let me die.' The plea might have come from either sex, it was too muffled by tears to tell.

'It was me.'

Jubal started, unaware that Holden had moved out onto the sidewalk. He believed that the albino meant to carry out his threat, but saw no reason to give himself up for a town too cowardly to defend itself. There were enough men lining the streets to take on Klein's gunmen. If the citizens weren't willing to fight for themselves, he wasn't about to offer himself up as a sacrificial lamb. Apparently, Holden felt differently.

'It was me. I killed them.'

'Who the hell are you?' Klein's voice was contemptuous. 'I didn't figger Angel to carry any heroes.'

'Name's Holden,' said the detective. 'Elias Holden. I work for the Pinkerton Agency. You kill me and you won't sleep too well. Pinkerton don't like his men shot, it upsets him. Means there's a standing price on the killer. Dead. Cost don't matter findin' him. Just so long as he pays.'

He stood on the edge of the boardwalk, to one side of a lamp, close to a beer barrel. He looked almost casual, thumbs hooked into his gunbelt, but Jubal could sense the tension in his figure, knew that the right hand was hooked looser than the left, ready to draw.

'That so?' Klein sounded calm, almost interested. 'I figure there's enough people want me dead that Pinkerton don't make too much difference.'

'Not so.' Holden was taking a long gamble, and he knew it. 'Pinkerton ain't people. The Agency's gonna hunt you like a dog if you kill me. Anyplace you go, you'll be lookin' over yore shoulder, wonderin'. They'll track you down an' kill you. That's a promise.'

'Makes me feel kinda wanted,' laughed Klein. 'So what's yore suggestion?'

'Ride out.' Holden eased his hand a little farther from his gunbelt. 'Take the bank. Whatever. But don't gun the town.'

Klein chuckled, easing the black horse around a little. The movement shifted him sideways on to Holden, his red eyes catching the full glow of the lamps so that they seemed to spark crimson fire from his death-white face.

'Guess not,' he murmured. And drew his gun.

Holden was fast. Very fast. He hauled his own revolver clear of the holster as he threw himself off the sidewalk. He loosed off one wild shot as he travelled through the air, seeking the cover of the nearest beer barrel. Klein was faster still. His gun came up in a blur of movement, spouting flame while Holden was still in mid-air. The bullet took the Pinkerton through the left knee, shattering the cap so that he screamed, and tumbled awkwardly behind the shelter of the keg. Clutching his broken leg with his left hand, he rolled behind cover, triggering a second shot. It blasted close by Klein's head, but the albino sat his horse almost casually, levelling the big Smith & Wesson on his target. He fired, and the shot spumed beer from the hole in the keg. The second drilled another hole through the wood, and Holden screamed as it ploughed on through his shoulder. He rolled out, fighting to aim his Remington on the albino. Klein smiled and fired again. The shot hit the Pinkerton between the eyes. It caved in the front of his face and blew away a fist-sized chunk of his skull. His body slammed down onto the sidewalk, the Remington discharging once as rictus tightened his nerve endings. The shot blew another hole in the beer keg.

Jubal watched as a long, amber fountain of liquid spouted from the keg. It curved out through the warm lamplight, falling into the hole that had once been Elias Holden's face. For a moment it appeared as though the skull would contain the flood, but then the hole filled up, spilling beer outwards over the torn flesh. It washed away the blood, dripping down into the open mouth, as though Holden's corpse sought one last drink before entering the land of eternal fountains.

Klein calmed his horse down, turning to level the S&W on Graves.

'Like we were sayin,' Vance. You got a way with words.'

'Jesus, Saul,' the sheriff's gut shook with fear, 'I never figgered it to be you.'

Jubal stayed in back of the saloon doors, listening. It was strange that Vance Graves should walk out into a street full of gunmen with the intention of stopping their carnage, then cower in abject terror at the appearance of Klein. He couldn't understand it, though, from the way they were talking, it sounded like they knew one another from way back. And didn't like the knowing.

'Who were you expecting?' Klein asked gently, the softness of his voice belying the undercurrent of menace. 'Jesse, maybe? Or Quantrill?'

Graves shook his head hopelessly, his multiple chins wobbling. Watching him, Jubal suddenly realized that the fat sheriff was crying. Fear had taken a firm hold on him, totally negating his earlier show of courage, reducing him to a tired, frightened old man. It was as though Klein had some kind of hold over him. Jubal glanced away to Holden's corpse, wondering what the fear stemmed from.

The spilled beer had filled the skull now, and was running all over the empty face. It was an ugly sight. Almost as ugly as the cringing of the lawman under the cold red stare of the albino killer.

'Weren't me, Saul.' Graves' voice was pitching higher now. 'I swear it. I give you my word. Not me.'

'Don't matter too much either way,' smiled Klein. 'You was part of it. There was no way that patrol could have found us without help. You always were an obliging kind of guy.'

'No!' Graves' voice, now, was a shout of naked fear. 'Not me. Not me, Saul. It was him. Him!'

The sheriff pointed over to the Kansas Palace, and the men outside shifted back, nervously. The front of the hotel was lit brilliantly, its wide glass doors pegged back to expose the faded plush of the interior. On either side of the doors stood Ives Brady's bodyguards, scatterguns pointed outwards. Brady was nowhere to be seen.

'Who, Vance?' Klein asked quietly. 'Them hired guns? The cowpokes?'

The fat man shook his head vigorously, beads of sweat spraying loose from his flabby face.

'Him, Saul. Brady. Ives Brady.' Graves stared wide-eyed at the albino, his jowls shuddering with fear. 'After we hit that payroll, it was him gave you away.'

'We'll talk about it.' The way Klein said it made the lawman's face wobble with raw terror.

The albino looked down the street. His men were positioned to destroy the entire town if he gave the word. Apart from a handful of citizens, and Jubal, the whole population of Angel and the outlying homesteads and ranches was gathered in the street, under the watchful guns of Klein's men. He motioned with his head, and the gunmen began herding people together, driving them like cattle to a central cluster. Klein shouted orders, and the citizens were herded towards the saloon. Jubal watched them approach, then moved silently back, making for the stairs. He reached the balcony and climbed the ladder to the roof. The night was cooling down, and the flat expanse of tar paper was dense with shadow. Carefully, he closed the trapdoor, then hunkered down beside the false frontage. He kept the Colt in his hand, ready to use, but mostly he was listening, wondering what personal vendetta had brought Saul Klein into the open.

The albino dismounted as the last of the townsfolk were ushered into the saloon. His men posted guards while others searched the buildings. Every one, bar the Kansas Palace.

Klein waited until he was sure he had all the citizens under watch, then called out to the big hotel.

'I know you're in there, Ives. You gonna come out, or do I come get you?'

There was no answer. Only the black muzzle of the bodyguards' shotguns.

Klein shrugged, dismounted. He tethered the big stallion on the far side of the street, taking care to place it out of range of the guns.

'All right, Ives. If that's how you want it.'

He waved an arm, and two of his men shoved Sheriff Graves out onto the boardwalk. They propelled him bodily, so that he lost his footing and pitched down into the street. He gasped as he felt the planks go from under him, then cried out as he hit the dirt. The two men followed him, hauling him up to a kneeling position and lashing his wrists tight to the hitching rail. When they were finished, the fat lawman had both arms spread wide, wrists corded to the pole so that he knelt in the dirt, head hung low and tears dripping from his flabby cheeks.

Klein lifted a bullwhip, looking across to the Kansas Palace. Henry and the other bodyguard were still posted by the door, their scatterguns deterring an attack. Klein smiled and swung the long, lead-weighted lash over Graves' shoulders. The lawman screamed.

'Up to you, Ives.' The albino brought the whip down again,

71

cutting a swathe of material from Graves' coat. 'Vance will tell me all about it. I'd just like to hear your side.' He lashed the bullwhip a third time and blood showed through the cuts in the cloth. 'One way or another, we'll get to the bones of it.'

Graves screamed as the whip cut him again.

CHAPTER SEVEN

With the terrified citizens corralled in the saloon, the riflemen came down from their vantage points. Jubal eased forwards, getting close to the edge of the flat roof. He had a clear view of the street below and could hear all that was said. For a while there was only the whistle of the bullwhip and the screaming.

Klein applied the plaited leather with brutal efficiency. It sliced through Graves' coat, cutting the material as cleanly as a knife. Soon the sheriff's jacket was cut into ribbons, hanging from his bleeding back in a series of long, stained streamers. His shirt was invisible beneath the welling blood, and the pale flesh of his back was rapidly crimsoned as a network of cuts erupted under the lash. Graves twisted awkwardly, trying to jerk away from the whipping, a continuous bellowing scream bursting from his open mouth. His arms were stretched out to either side, roped firm to the hitching rail, and all he could do was heave his gross body from side to side in a hopeless attempt to escape the pain.

Klein kept it up until the lawman's head sank down onto his chest and the screaming died away to a low whimpering. Then the albino looked up, staring across the street at the door of the Kansas Palace.

'You gonna watch me flay him, Ives? Ain't you gonna try to stop me?'

There was no answer.

'I'll kill him, Ives.' The finality in his voice left no doubt. 'But first he's gonna tell these good citizens all about their golden-haired Senator. You want that, Ives? You gonna hide behind those scatterguns, or you gonna come out an' face me?'

The hotel remained silent. Brady's bodyguards were hoping

73

for a stand-off. They knew their shotguns couldn't carry effectively to Klein's position, and realized that a shot would bring down a barrage of fire from Klein's men. The best they could hope for was that the heavy weapons would deter the raiders from launching a head-on attack.

'OK, Ives,' Klein shouted, coiling the bullwhip, 'if that's how you want it.'

He stepped over to Graves' sagging body and grabbed the sheriff's hair. Callously, he yanked the head back, grinning as he saw the rolling eyes and gaping mouth.

'Now you can tell them, Vance. Tell them all about Ives Brady an' his jayhawking days.'

He called for someone to bring water, and a grinning man with one eye covered by a patch carried a bucket from the Laughing Lady. He up-ended the contents over Vance Graves and the sheriff shook his head like a beaten dog.

'Go ahead, Vance,' Klein urged. 'Tell them.'

He pulled a switchblade from his coat pocket and hacked through the bindings. Graves fell clear of the hitching rail, flopping face-down in the dirt with blood oozing over his heaving shoulders.

'Tell them, Vance!' Klein hauled the man to his feet, spinning him round to face the saloon. 'Bring them out! I want everyone to hear this.'

The gunmen prodded the townspeople to the front of the saloon where they huddled like sheep caught in a blizzard, nervous of the levelled guns. They watched the tottering figure of Graves, caught between horror at his suffering and curiosity. Then, slowly, the lawman began to speak.

'Was back before the war. We was kids then, not much past sixteen or so. Ives,' he nodded over his shoulder, 'he was the oldest. You all know his folks came from these parts, same as you know I was raised on a dirt farm not more'n ten miles from here. Saul, he was off a Mormon wagon train. Run away after beatin' up on his old man when he threatened to whip the boy.'

He paused, shoulders slumped in resignation. The town was

very quiet, listening, wondering. Graves voice carried through the silence, husked though it was by pain.

'We helled around together. Three kids on the prod, lookin' fer excitement. We found it when the slavery thing got started. Ives, an' Saul an' me, we was jayhawkers right from the start. Harpers Ferry lit us up good. Like givin' a quarter-horse the off.'

Jubal listened from the roof. He had heard of the Kansas jayhawkers: bands of armed men who had taken it upon themselves to carry out a private war even before the great struggle between North and South got started. Crazy John Brown had begun hacking men down at Pottawatomie Creek in 1856, expressing in blood his wild-eyed views on slavery. After that, a savage border war started up, with kill-happy raiders from both sides of the argument shooting up the territory. The guerrilla fighting gave Kansas a title that stuck: Bleeding Kansas.

When the Civil War broke out – officially – the jayhawkers mostly joined whichever side they favoured. Some, with the taste for blood strong in their mouths, became freelance raiders, like the infamous Quantrill. In the main, both sides despised them, recognizing their rapaciousness for the lawless savagery it was.

If Ives Brady had been one of those killers, his political career was finished as soon as word got out.

Graves' voice intruded on his thoughts: 'We figgered we was doin' right. We got a bunch o' good old boys together an' set to raidin' the Southron sympathizers. Thought to be supportin' the Union. Only it went wrong someplace along the line. Seemed like all of a sudden we was hittin' anything that took our fancy. Ives was our leader – he was always the one with the brains – an' he took us to them places that appeared to carry the most money. After a while, we didn't bother any more about joinin' up. Just settled in to raidin'. Like Quantrill, I guess.'

Klein was smiling now, staring hard towards the open door of the Kansas Palace, revelling in the violent opening of forgotten sores. Behind him, in the saloon, there was the rustle of surprised voices, the townsfolk remembering the vicious jay-hawking days.

'Tell them about the payroll, Vance,' prompted the albino. 'How ole Ives set that one up.'

'We got word,' said the fat man, 'of a big payroll goin' through to Fort Larned. Ives told us about it. Was him planned the whole thing. First off, we ambushed a Union patrol. Hit them down near the Deadman creek an' wiped them out. We took their uniforms and waited fer the pay wagons to come on through.'

The town was quiet again, straining to catch the words, shocked that the representative of the law should prove an outlaw killer with a violent record.

'They come by real easy,' continued Graves, 'an' we rode out to meet them like we was genuine bluecoats. We got up close an' started in to firin'. Was like a turkey shoot: they weren't expectin' no ambuscade from their own colour. We killed them all an' then took the money. After that we headed back to Deadman Crossing. We hid our trail pretty good, but those rocks are hard to get to, anyway. We coulda held off an army if the need had arisen. It didn't though: war was goin' too busy fer the North to spare troops on a hunt. We just sat tight an' split the proceeds. It came to quite a bit, an' Ives took the lion's share on account o' he planned it all.'

For a moment, the man's voice broke, snuffling off into silence as though he was suddenly embarrassed by the past he had kept hidden for so long.

'Tell the rest of it,' urged Klein. 'Right down to the happy ending.'

'Ain't too much more,' muttered Graves. 'You know that, Saul.'

'Folks here don't,' smiled the albino. 'So you spell it out for them. All the way.'

'Sure,' shrugged Graves, 'why not? We split the money an' decided to separate. We didn't know then the Union couldn't afford to send men after us, an' we was gettin' worried with all that money in our pockets. We agreed to divide up, maybe meet later. Never did, though. I guess we all rode away intendin' to forget the deal.

'Me, I got down to Texas. Bought in to a small spread. Then the war ended an' I figgered I was safe. Only the ranch dried up an' I lost everythin'. Come on back to Angel an' took the badge. Wasn't no one else willin' an' I was a might more sprightly then. The rest you know.

'Ives, he dropped outta sight fer a while. Next time I heard o' him, he was into politics. Elected Senator an' all.

'Saul I never saw no more. Until today.'

'You left a part out.' Klein's voice cut like the lash of the bullwhip. 'The important part. The reason I'm here now. Tell them about the money, Vance. Tell them what happened to it.'

'Jesus, Saul!' Graves' voice lifted to a quavering tremolo and his heavy head shook from side to side. 'What do you want? Blood?'

'Yeah,' rasped Klein. 'An' I'm gonna get it. Tell them, Vance. The whole story.'

'We took around thirty thousand dollars.' Graves' eyes were closed now, his head bowed. But his voice carried clearly through the stillness. 'After splittin' with the others I had three grand. So did Ives an' Saul. Them two never did get on that well, an' afore we rode out Ives put a proposition to me. He said we should lay up fer Saul an' take his share. We was both Kansas born, he wasn't. Guess that's what made the difference. Anyway, we all rode out in different directions. Only Ives an' me, we circled round to meet up. Then we waited fer Saul. When he come along we ambuscaded him an' took his money.

'I lost mine like I tole you. Ives, he went on to use his in politics. That's where his backin' come from: stolen Union payroll.'

Klein chuckled, watching the crowd. Fear was partly stilled now, replaced by amazement and anger. Graves stood with tears running down his cheeks and blood welling from his lacerated back. Years of respectability were gone in one bloody night of remembrance; the risks taken as sheriff, the friendships he had built, all were wiped out in the violent recollection of his wild days. He looked as though he might welcome death.

'You tell a real nice story, Vance,' said Klein, softly. 'An' because you did, I'm gonna make things easy for you.'

He tossed the bullwhip out into the street, keeping his back to the Kansas Palace. Casually, he drew his gun. He pulled the hammer back and levelled the Smith & Wesson at Graves' head.

'I'm gonna kill you, but I'll do it fast. You'll get it a whole lot easier than Brady.'

Graves turned his head, and there was no hope in his eyes. There was no fear any more either. The blank, blue orbs looked as though all feeling had gone from them, leaving behind only a great weariness that bordered on resignation. Slowly, coursing through the dust on his face, tears ran down his flabby cheeks. Half-naked, his coat and shirt hanging in tatters around his belly, he looked a pathetic figure.

Klein raised his arm, extending the gun so that it came close to touching Graves' face. The fat sheriff didn't move, just stared down the muzzle.

'So long, Vance,' said the albino. And squeezed the trigger.

At that close range, the .44 slug should have killed Graves instantly. But it didn't. Whether it was deliberate or not, Jubal couldn't decide. From the roof it looked as though Klein shifted his aim at the last moment, dropping the S&W to line on the sheriff's mouth. The albino was enough of a sadist to play a final cat-and-mouse game to add to the lawman's suffering, and Jubal thought the move was most likely intentional. Either way, it laid an extra burden of pain on Graves' bloody shoulders.

The bullet entered his mouth between the parted, panting lips. It travelled on past his teeth to rip through the soft membranes of his throat. Passing through the flesh, it hit the vertebrae of his spine, shattering several small sections of bone together with the nerve linkages running through and around the column of bone. From the back of Graves' neck there exploded a great bloody fragment of flesh. The sheriff's head snapped back and his knees appeared to fold up, so that he sat down heavily. Reflex action lifted his hands to the flow of scarlet pulsing from his throat, and he tried to say something. The words wouldn't form and all he did was make a rumbling, throaty sound that urged a fresh welling of blood from the wound. It spilled over his lips, dribbling to his chest, and he raised one hand, staring vacantly at the sticky red mess covering the palm.

Then he tilted his head back, peering at Klein. Painfully, forming the words with agonizing care, he spoke.

'You always was a mean bastard, Saul.'

'I ain't changed,' said Klein.

He stood, watching Graves, as the fat man's eyes grew blurred, clouding over with the realization of death. Slowly, the big hands went down by his sides and he began to lean forwards. He doubled over until his head was touching the street and the noises in his throat stopped. After a while the blood stopped spurting too.

Klein looked up. 'Now you know the truth about yore sheriff an' yore Senator. Now you know why I'm here.'

The townsfolk seemed to draw closer together under the red stare. Klein laughed, turning back to the Kansas Palace.

'Now what, Ives? Vance always did have a big mouth. I guess he's shot it off for the last time.'

CHAPTER EIGHT

Jubal waited for the next move. His watch showed fifteen minutes after midnight and the frontage of the Kansas Palace remained as bright and silent as ever. The bodies of the shot townsfolk still decorated the street, and Vance Graves was slumped alongside the hitching rail, his bloody back looking dark in the lanterns' light.

Klein was standing, waiting for Brady to reply, with the S&W held negligently in one hand.

'If you don't come out, I'll hafta come in.' His voice sounded almost casual.

'Try it!' Henry answered for Brady. 'You'll be chewin' on buckshot.'

Klein nodded slowly, smiling. Then he turned and crossed to his horse. He lifted the Winchester from the saddle boot and climbed onto the sidewalk. Motioning his men to get the people back inside the saloon, he stood for a moment, watching the hotel. Abruptly, he threw the rifle to his shoulder and squeezed off a shot. Half the glass in one side of the hotel's grandiose door exploded inwards. There was a scream and the thud of a falling body. Henry shouted something and triggered the scattergun. The blast was impressive, but the buckshot didn't carry far enough to harm Klein who was levering a second shell into the breech of the rifle. He peered through the telescopic sight, fiddled with the adjusting screws, then fired again.

The other side of the door shattered, and Jubal saw the crouched figure of Ives Brady dart across the vestibule. A moment later Henry shouted from inside.

'I'll make a deal. My life for Brady. How's it sound?'

'Reasonable,' hollered Klein. 'Send him out, then come out yoreself.'

Jubal could see the bodyguard retreat inside the hotel. A moment later Brady was propelled outwards, staggering across the sidewalk with his hands raised. Henry followed him, scattergun levelled on the Senator's back.

Klein smiled, holding the Winchester casually across his hips. He waited until Brady had stepped down into the street, walking nervously towards the albino, then swung the rifle round and up. It was a movement almost too fast to follow, certainly too fast for Henry. Klein fired from the hip, the shot slamming the bodyguard back into the broken glass of the hotel's door. He shouted once, the cry drowned out by the detonation of the scattergun, then a second bullet hit him and he arced over the half-frame of the door. For a moment, his boots drummed against the wood, loosening a snowfall of broken glass that tumbled over his bleeding chest. Then he was quiet.

Klein laughed, holding the Winchester on Brady. 'You don't pick yore guards too well, Ives. Maybe you shoulda paid them more. You got the money for it.'

Brady didn't reply. From where Jubal watched, it looked like he was too scared. His carefully groomed hair was in disarray, and the front of his white suit was dirtied where he had jumped from the wagon. His necktie was dragged loose, and his mouth set in a tight line that couldn't hide the trembling of his lips. His eyes, wide and staring, were fixed on the muzzle of Klein's rifle.

The albino watched him approach, a wide, evil smile on his thin-featured face.

'You an' me, we got a whole lot o' talkin' to do, Ives.' His tone halted the politician in his tracks. 'Reckon we'll take our time over it.'

He turned, shouting into the saloon. Three men came out and set off up the street. After a while they returned, leading a string of horses. Klein motioned for Brady to mount, then called out to the remaining gunmen. They backed out of the Laughing Lady and closed the doors with an upturned beer barrel. Klein studied the saloon for a moment.

'Don't know how you folks feel about all this,' he grinned, 'but I wouldn't advise you to try followin' us. Anyone who does is likely to wind up dead. Were I in yore position, I'd sit tight for an hour or so.'

He turned the black stallion on its heels and led the way out of Angel. Jubal waited until the cavalcade reached the end of mainstreet, then stood up. Peering through the darkness, he could just make out their direction. Southwest towards Deadman Crossing. He slid the Colt into the shoulder holster and crossed to the trapdoor. Inside, the Laughing Lady was a hubbub of noise. It stopped briefly as Jubal came down the stairs, ignoring the curious looks he was getting, then started up again as he shouldered his way to the door. A storekeeper tried to stop him, demanding to know what he was doing, who he was.

'Name's Cade,' grunted Jubal, setting his shoulder to the barrel. 'I aim to find Klein.'

No one volunteered to help him, though some cowboys helped shift the keg and announced their intention of riding over to Ellsworth to hunt up some law. It suited Jubal: if Klein was holding Andy in the hideout, a posse would only stir things up. Tracking Saul Klein and getting the boy was a one-man job. It never even crossed his mind to try rescuing Brady.

The bay horse was well rested and comfortably fed. Jubal took a sack of oats from the store-room behind the livery and stashed it on his saddle. He raided the kitchen of the hotel for supplies, stowing salt pork, beans and coffee in a gunny sack that balanced the oats on his saddle, and took off into the night.

The moon had come up, high and bright, lighting the trail near as well as day. For the first hour it was clear to follow. It went southwest on a path straight as a section of good railroad, crossing the plains in the direction of the Arkansas River. After that it got harder to follow, swinging away to the east where a section of rocky ground blotted out the hoofprints. Jubal cast around for almost an hour before he was forced to

82

admit the tracks were lost and climbed down off the big bay horse. He hunkered down, letting the pony take a breather while he thought about his next move.

Locating the trail again, even given the moon's light, would be a time-consuming chore. Going back to Angel was pretty pointless: Klein would have cut the telegraph wires, so any messages from Agnew would be delayed longer than the waiting was worth. That left one possibility. Both Holden and Graves had talked about Deadman Crossing. If Klein had used the place in his jayhawking days, the chances were that he would head back there now. Jubal reviewed what he knew of the location. It was on the Arkansas, Holden had said, a range of hills cut through by a stream. Cliffs on both sides and caves aplenty, one of them containing Klein and his men. Hopefully, Andy too, if he was lucky.

Jubal flexed his arms, preparing for a long ride. The dead Pinkerton had said the hideout was three days' ride to the southwest. It was Jubal's best bet, and he wanted to get there ahead of Klein if he could.

He mounted up and heeled the bay horse to a mile-eating canter across the empty Kansas plain.

The bay was a willing animal, long-legged and deep-chested, with the graceful lines of a quarterhorse mingled with the staying power of a mustang. But even its proud strength faltered as the sun came up and began to heat the prairie. Jubal himself was dog-tired, his ribs and side aching, his limbs stiffening from the long chase. Reluctantly, he bowed to common sense and reined the horse in by a small creek. He hobbled its forelegs and unshipped the saddle before rubbing the animal down and feeding it. He didn't bother to eat himself, just spread his bedroll and collapsed into sleep with the sun heating his face and a cicada serenading his ears.

The same insect, or a close relative, was playing its castanet rhythm when he awoke. Glancing at the gold Hunter, he saw the time was close on nine. He had slept longer than he intended, and his breakfast was consequently briefer. Coffee and biscuits reminded him that he had not eaten the night before, but he ignored his hunger as he ignored the dull ache in his side. He wished that Holden had given him some kind of map: he was unfamiliar with the territory and had no sure way of knowing where the old jayhawker hideout was situated.

His best course, he decided, was to keep heading southwest until he struck the hills. Then he would have to quarter them until he found the crossing.

Throughout the long, hot day he held the bay horse to a fast pace. Every so often, wary of winding the animal, he dismounted and walked a quarter-mile or so. He was riding when the settlement showed, and turned the big animal towards the lights.

The buildings huddled beside a wide track that sliced arrow-straight across the plain and disappeared off into the night. There was a big corral and a barn, a low wooden building that looked like a bunkhouse, and a stone-built cantina. When Jubal got up close enough to read the peeling sign hung outside, he learned the place was a way-station for the stage line. There was a decrepit feeling to the cluster of shacks, as though few stages came by and the whole outfit was running down. A dog began to bark, and by the time Jubal was on the ground a man was standing outside the cantina, light pooling around him from the lantern he was holding.

'Can I stable my horse?' Jubal asked.

'In there.' The man gestured at the barn. 'You'll find hay an' a well out back. Dollar-fifty a night, you an' the pony.'

'Sure,' nodded Jubal, leading the horse towards the barn.

He bedded the animal down, noticing that three other horses were already in the booths, and made for the cantina. He took his medical bag and the Spencer with him.

Inside, the place was fractionally better than its exterior. But only just. The walls were of unpainted adobe, narrow windows shuttered against the night. Light came from several kerosene lamps hung from the low ceiling, their yellow flames attracting a crowd of suicidal moths. A long bar, made up from sections of planking set on barrels, ran down one wall and a pot-belly stove, unlit, occupied the centre of the room. Around the dirt floor there were tables and chairs. Three chairs were occupied.

The men looked up as Jubal came in, studying him with the calculated casualness of men accustomed to looking out for dangerous strangers. Jubal recognized one of them: the man with the eye patch who had poured water over Vance Graves back in Angel. Better lit now, the man looked uglier than ever. His good eye was a watery blue that reminded Jubal of a dying fish. His hollowed cheeks were covered with a stubble of black beard that served to emphasize the dirty yellow of his tobacco-stained teeth. He was dressed in a grubby linen shirt and broadcloth pants held up by the same belt that supported his holstered Colt .45.

His companions looked little better. One was a middle-aged man, balding and bearded, a corncob pipe clenched tight between his teeth. He wore a farmer's Sunday suit stretched taut across his beefy shoulders, the tails dragged back to expose the butt of a .44 Remington Army model revolver. The other was considerably younger, most likely still in his teens. He affected a flowing moustache in an attempt to look older, and his grey eyes had a nervousness lacking in those of his companions. He was dressed in worn, but clean denims, an ivory-handled S&W American hung on his belt.

Jubal nodded a greeting, concealing his excitement. He hadn't expected to come across the gang so soon, but – unless they had split up – these three could lead him to Klein. Suddenly, his impatience at having to stop for food and rest evaporated: it was a lucky break.

'Gents.' He tipped the grey derby as he crossed to the bar.

They murmured a disinterested reply and went back to their cards. Jubal ordered a whiskey and lit a cheroot, leaning casually on the planking as the station manager filled a shot glass.

'If you come to sell me anythin', you're pure out o' luck.' He glanced at Jubal's clothes. 'Ain't a thing I want.'

Jubal grinned. It wasn't the first time he had been taken for a drummer.

'I'm not selling anything,' he said quietly. 'Just passing through.'

The man ran a grubby hand over his thinning hair, his narrow-lipped mouth drooping with a mixture of resignation and defiance. His eyes, set deep into a sallow face, looked tired. As he wiped the bar his shoulders slumped.

'Good.' Even his voice sounded weary. 'Ain't no point to buyin' no more.'

'How come?' Jubal wanted to get a conversation going, steer it around to the three men behind him.

'Line's closin',' grunted the bartender. 'We don't get more'n two coaches a week through since the railroad opened up. Ain't worth keepin' this place goin'. Leastways, that's what they tell me.'

'How about riders?' Jubal asked. 'They need a road house, don't they?'

'Riders?' The man snorted. 'Them an' you are the first folks I seen inside a seven-day. People head north to Angel, or cut around to Danceville. They don't come through here no more.'

Jubal turned his head, looking over the cardplayers. 'You got people in tonight.'

The stationman shrugged. 'I got lucky.'

'You hear about Angel?' Jubal kept his voice casual, idly gossiping. He wanted to stir the outlaws a bit, just enough to speed them on their way to the hideout. 'I heard it got held up. Bunch of riders came in and shot up the place. Then they took Senator Brady.'

'That so?' The station manager didn't sound particularly interested.

'You talk an awful lot, mister.'

The statement came from Jubal's left side and he looked round to see the one-eyed man standing beside him. The boy came up on his right, and he could sense the farmer-type behind him. One-eye grinned as he reached out to pat Jubal's

86

side, feeling the bulk of the shoulder holster beneath the coat.

'Like I thought: a side gun.' He grinned, exhaling bad breath. 'Only folks I know that carry them are gamblers and Pinkertons. You ain't a gambler 'cos you're too far off the money routes. Guess that makes you a Pinkerton.'

Jubal shook his head. 'No. I'm a doctor.'

'An' I'm the President,' laughed the outlaw. 'What the hell would a doctor be doin' out here? Why'd a sawbones carry a gun?'

'For protection,' said Jubal evenly. 'I heard there were some rough types in Kansas.'

Then he hit the man. He brought his left arm back in a short, stabbing motion that rammed viciously into the outlaw's midriff. One-eye groaned, clutching at his winded stomach. Jubal brought his right arm off the bar, spilling the contents of his glass into the youngster's face. The boy yelled as the home-brewed whiskey scalded his eyes and dropped the gun he was pulling. The oldest of the three was coming up from behind, and Jubal dropped both hands onto the planking of the bar, using his arms like springs to power himself backwards.

He cannoned into the raider, his weight rocking the bigger man back on his heels. Still facing away, Jubal stamped his right heel down over the man's foot. The outlaw bellowed as the full force of Jubal's boot smashed against the delicate bones. Jubal pivoted, grinding down, and launched himself at the one-eyed man.

The boy was still out of the fight, rubbing at eyes that streamed tears where the whiskey had burned them; and the old man was too busy nursing his broken foot to join in for a while. Jubal concentrated on the third killer.

One-eye was reaching for the Colt on his waist when Jubal grabbed him. His arms were knocked out on either side as powerful fingers clamped tight around his wrists. Then he was yanked forwards as Jubal bent his knees and let himself fall backwards. He raised one foot, planting it against the outlaw's belly, and pushed as he fell back. The man with the eye patch

87

yelped like a September hog as he was lifted up into the air. He rose vertically, propelled by Jubal's outthrust leg, then pivoted, toppling over against his middle-aged sidekick. Both men fell to the floor, but as the one-eyed outlaw went down Jubal retained the grip on his wrists. The man screamed as his right arm dislocated, snapping from the shoulder socket with a dull *click*.

Jubal rolled away from the sprawled figures in time to see the kid aiming a kick at his head. He flattened against the dirt floor, letting the boot swing above his face. Then he reached up to grab the ankle and twist savagely. Turned off balance, the boy gasped, flailing his arms in a desperate attempt to stay on his remaining foot. Jubal pulled, and he toppled over, slamming heavily against the bar as he went down.

Jubal lifted to his feet, reaching for his gun. The one-eyed man was huddled on the floor, moaning as he clutched at his useless arm. The big man in the farmer's suit was sitting up, massaging his damaged foot, one eye closed where the flying body had caught him. The youngster was out of it, unconscious. Jubal grinned, feeling the tension ease from his face, and levelled the Colt.

Then something poked him in the back and a weary voice rang in his ear.

'Put the gun away, mister.' It was the stationman. 'I ain't about to see you kill 'em cold.'

'How'd you know I would?' Jubal asked.

'Maybe you wasn't plannin' to,' admitted the man, 'but then again, maybe you was. Either way it comes to the same. I ain't had no real excitement in too damn' long. Now I'm gonna organize me some.'

He chuckled: Jubal didn't like the sound of it.

'We're gonna have ourselves a gunfight. You, friend, are gonna shoot it out with them.'

'All three?' Jubal said. 'You want a gunfight or a massacre?'

'Look at it this way,' grinned the balding man. 'You already beat 'em in a fist fight. There's two crippled an' the kid's knocked halfway crazy. That should even up the odds. Course, if you still don't like 'em, there's always this.'

Jubal turned and found himself looking down the muzzles of a 12-gauge Meteor. Both hammers were all the way back and the station manager looked like he knew how to use the shotgun. Jubal stared at him, weighing his chances. Refusal to go along with the man's crazy plan meant no chance at all; but a three-against-one gunfight wasn't too appealing either. On the other hand, the one-eyed man would find it hard to use his right arm, even if someone set it for him, and the big farmer-type obviously couldn't stand on his damaged foot. That brought the odds down. The youngster was coming to, and in a while would be fit to fight; so the sooner Jubal got it done, the better.

He could feel his anger stretching the skin taut over his cheek-bones as he nodded to the balding man, and his answer came out harsh and bitter.

'All right. I guess I don't have a choice.'

'Bella!' The man called over his shoulder. 'Come on out here!'

'What is it?' The woman who emerged from the rear room was one of the ugliest Jubal had ever seen. 'What you playin' at, Monte?'

The man explained quickly and the woman's pasty face split in an ugly smile. She was fat, and her face was marked with the scars of smallpox. Tiny blue eyes peered out from between wobbling folds of surplus skin that advertised the fact her cook stove smoked a lot. Her hair was blond and stringy, matted with grease. The stains on her dress suggested that bathing was not one of her favourite pastimes.

But the ugliest thing about her was the unhidden sadism in her laugh.

She ducked back into the other room, emerging with a pitcher of water. The youngster howled and jumped to his feet when she tipped it over his head, but Bella only laughed again and picked up a second scattergun.

She held it on the room while Monte stepped out from

behind the bar to explain his maniac plan. The outlaws looked near as shocked as Jubal. Then cheered up when they figured the odds. Still shaking his head, the kid took hold of One-eye's wrist and braced a foot against his armpit. The older man screamed as his limb was jumped back into its socket, but then he stood up, glowering at Jubal. Aided by the boy, he got the big man on his feet, propping him against the stove. Monte retrieved the fallen revolver and handed it to the kid. Then he stepped back behind the bar.

'Now back off, mister.' He pointed his shotgun at Jubal. 'You move back ten paces.'

Jubal followed the orders.

'I'm gonna count to three. Then you all draw. Anyone tries to jump the gun, he'll be cut down where he stands. Anyone tries to run,' he looked at Jubal, 'I'll kill him. Them as lives gets drinks on the house.'

Beside him, Bella beamed, delighting in the drama. Her piggy eyes darted avidly from one side of the room to the other, anxious not to miss anything. Monte sipped his own whiskey, his tired eyes suddenly awake with excitement.

'One!'

Jubal tensed, using his left hand to hold his coat out away from his holster.

'Two!'

One-eye hiked his holster around to his left hip. The big man leaned against the stove, freeing his right arm for use. The kid wet his lips, bending his knees the way someone had told him real gunfighters do it.

'Three!'

Jubal powered sideways as the sentence ended, his Colt clearing the holster while he was still in the air. He hit a table, crashing it over as two bullets ploughed the empty space where he had stood. One-eye was slower, fumbling his gun out with his left hand. The big man was having trouble balancing on his one good foot. That made the boy Jubal's first target.

He felt a slug hit the table as the kid fanned his gun, throwing wild lead all over the cantina, and rolled away. He was belly-down on the dirt floor while the boy was still slapping his hammer. Until Jubal's bullet hit him in the throat. It blew his Adam's apple out the back of his neck and he dropped the Smith & Wesson, trying to scream and staunch the wound at the same time.

Jubal's second shot took the big man in the farmer's suit through the belly. It doubled him over with blood coming out of his mouth, and he began to writhe on the floor like a stranded fish.

One-eye loosed off a shot that would have hit had Jubal stayed in the same position. But he was rolling over the dirt, shifting his position. He kicked a chair aside, ignoring the splinters blasted across his face by the outlaw's second bullet, and took careful aim.

In some ways the one-eyed raider was lucky: Jubal still wanted a guide to the hideout. In others he was less fortunate: Jubal's shot was aimed to maim without killing. It hit on the right side of his body, halfway down the rib cage. A rib broke under the impact, deflecting the lead slug off into the man's stomach where it tore a further hole through to his back, lodging finally against a second rib, close under his shoulder-blades. The force of the blow lifted him off his feet, hurling him back over a table. He landed heavily, crashing to the ground as the table overturned. He tried to push himself up, then moaned once and slumped flat, unconscious.

The big man was still groaning softly beside the stove, both hands pressed tight to his bleeding belly. A slow, steady welling of blood ran through his clenched fingers; the flood coming out of the exit wound in his back was much greater. But he couldn't reach round there.

The kid was still on his feet, both hands wrapped around his throat as though he was trying to strangle himself. His face was several shades paler and there was a lot of blood on his moustache. As Jubal watched him, he gave one choking cry and pitched over. His chest heaved for a few seconds, then gave up the unequal struggle and ceased pumping.

Jubal climbed to his feet, holding the Colt. Rage had drawn

the skin of his face tight, emphasizing the pale scar tissue across his nose. His lips were thinned out, taut above his gritted teeth, and his eyes blazed above flared nostrils.

The ghastly fury jolted Monte's watchfulness a fraction of a second too long. Jubal triggered the Colt as he came upright, a snarl of animalistic rage breaking from his lips. The bullet took Monte dead centre of his chest. It picked him up and threw him back against the shelves behind the bar. Two lengths of timber broke when he hit them, spilling bottles onto the floor as his shotgun blasted a hole through the roof. Jubal was powering back and to the side as he fell, diving for the cover of a table. Bella's gun went off with a roar like a Fourth of July cannon, and Jubal felt the table pitch back under the impact. He kicked it forwards, rolling away as the second barrel exploded 12-gauge shot in his direction. It ploughed a dirty furrow across the floor, and the fat woman began to curse as she realized that she had missed.

Jubal came up on his feet, the Colt pointed at the woman. He had one bullet left. And he was ready to use it on her.

'Drop it!' His voice was harsh with anger.

Bella looked up from the carton of buckshot. When she saw Jubal's face she dropped the Meteor and began to cry. The tears looked out of place on her ugly features. She knelt down behind the bar, cradling Monte's head in her flabby arms. Jubal glanced around the smoke-filled room and decided he had time to reload. Fast and deft, he snapped the loading gate of the Peacemaker open and began to work the ejector rod to discharge the spent shells. He shoved fresh cartridges into five of the revolver's chambers, settling the hammer on the empty sixth.

Monte groaned from behind the bar.

'Oh, Jesus! Bella, he's killed me.'

When Jubal went over to pick up the scatterguns he saw blood coming from Monte's mouth and nostrils: his shot had punctured a lung. Bella was busy mopping the blood with a corner of her dirty dress. Neither of them was fit to give trouble anymore. Jubal turned to the outlaws. The kid and the farmer-type were both stone-dead; One-eye was unconscious, his grubby shirt staining brown as blood pulsed from the wound over his ribs. Jubal lifted him, checking for an exit wound. There was none, only an ominous lump under his left shoulder that Jubal guessed was the lead slug. He felt over the broken rib, charting the course of the bullet through the man's body. The one-eyed outlaw had sustained severe internal injuries that would kill him in about thirty hours without medical attention. Jubal grinned and turned to the station manager and his wife.

Bella was still cradling her husband's blood-flecked face in her arms, slow tears coursing down her greasy cheeks. Monte was breathing with difficulty, each choking breath producing a thick flow of blood. The woman looked up as Jubal came over.

'Can you do anything?'

Jubal shook his head. 'No. He's dying.'

'You bastard!' Bella's voice was pure poison. 'You killed him.'

'Lady,' murmured Jubal, 'he set this thing up. He got what he deserved. Don't expect me to cry over him.'

Monte coughed a sticky gobbet of bright blood over his wife's arms and jerked once. Then he went stiff. Jubal didn't see it because he was busy in the back room looking for water. He found a stove with a kettle bubbling away like the froth coming out of One-eye's stomach, and set to hunting up rags and bowls. When he had what he wanted he went back into the bar. Bella was cradling Monte's body in her arms still, a low keening bursting from her fat lips.

'I need your help.' Jubal's voice was flat and calm. 'I can save one of them, but I have to operate now.'

'Go to hell!' Bella grunted through her tears. 'Why should I help you?'

'Because I'll kill you if you don't.' Jubal stared down at the fat woman, his lips thinned out, the rage still showing on his face.

Bella nodded without speaking, climbing wearily to her

93

feet. Fear showed in her pale eyes and she listened studiously to Jubal's instructions, hurrying to follow them. Jubal went back to the one-eyed man and lifted him up, setting him on the planking of the bar. He cut his shirt loose, using the remnants as a pillow. The medical valise was still on the floor and he opened it, extracting the instruments he would need. Bella brought hot water and began to clean the scalpels and probes as Jubal instructed. Jubal himself concentrated on cleaning the area of skin around the entry wound, then turned the man over on his stomach to prepare for the incision in his back. He could clean the man up and remove the bullet, patch him enough to live a few days longer, but after that the chances were that One-eye would die. A few days, though, were all Jubal needed: just sufficient for the man to lead him to Klein.

He injected morphine to kill the pain and then, aided by his unwilling nurse, began to remove the slug.

He cut a hole through the flesh beneath the outlaw's shoulder and inserted the probe. One-eye screamed as it went in, bucking high against the pain. Bella held him down, using her bulk to jam his face and shoulders onto the bar. Jubal located the slug and withdrew the slender length of the probe. He took a set of thin-tined tweezers from the hot water bowl and dug into the hole. The outlaw passed out. Thinking about the way medical training could be wasted, Jubal got the tweezers around the bullet. He felt the metal tips touch the slug and squeezed them together, gripping the thing. Then, gently, he withdrew the lead from the man's body. Fresh blood welled out as the slug came clear, and Jubal dropped the flattened metal to the floor. He bathed the wound and sealed it with lint from his medical bag. Then he did the same for the entry wound. After that he strapped the broken rib and left the killer to sleep.

He cleaned his instruments, setting each one carefully in its pocket within the bag, and washed his hands and face. Then he poured himself a whiskey and waited for the man to come around.

94

The way-station was thick now with flies. Even though Jubal's watch told him it was almost four in the morning, the busy insects concentrated on their unexpected feast. Bella helped him drag the bodies outside, seeming almost glad to have a man tell her what to do. Together they settled the outlaw as comfortably as possible without moving him, then Jubal suggested food.

The woman produced a stew that tasted almost as bad as it looked, but Jubal was too tired to worry. He watched Bella as he ate, then went out to toss the collected guns far away into the dying night. After that he found a room with a lock and shut her inside before making up a bed in the bunkhouse.

He woke with the sun on his face and the hungry dog barking at the door. When he looked at the corpses he decided the dog couldn't be so hungry anymore and ignored it. He opened Bella's room and went on to check the outlaw. The man was still alive and breathing stronger, so Jubal organized some broth, spooning it down the raider's throat before getting him dressed and saddling two horses. Bella came out of her room looking as ugly as ever, though now she was smiling.

'Where we heading for?'

Jubal looked at her. Her face was painted up, over the grease, and she simpered like a girl with her first beau. She was waiting for an answer she was afraid to hear, one that Jubal knew he would never give.

'I'm taking him.' The statement was flat and definite, accompanied by a motion towards the supine figure on the bar. 'South. I don't know about you.'

Bella twirled around, spreading the tattered hem of her best dress in a circle that exposed a flabby expanse of white thigh. She curtsied, displaying a panoramic view of pasty breasts.

'You're gonna take me with you.'

It was – oddly – a statement.

Jubal shook his head. 'No. I'm not.'

He watched the painted smile dissolve into grief and rage, thwarted purpose mingling with lost hope. The pancaked cosmetics plastered over her face split into the natural folds of loose flesh as she began to weep.

'You hafta take me. What can I do here? Monte's dead an' I can't run the place on my own. You gotta take me.'

'Lady,' said Jubal slowly, 'you were happy to see me killed. Don't expect any favours. I guess you need the next stage out. Otherwise you're on your own.'

Bella slumped into a chair. Her gross body shook as she accepted the realization of her loss, tears flooding down the fat cheeks. Jubal ignored her, checking over the one-eyed outlaw for complications in his rough surgery. The man was still breathing, indeed he seemed stronger, so Jubal brought two horses around to the front and lifted him into a saddle, tying him in place. The last thing he saw of the lonely way-station was Bella, slumped fatly over the verandah with flies buzzing around her eyes.

Ignoring the woman, he steered towards the southwest, leading the other horse behind. The one-eyed man hung over the saddle, held on mostly by the restraining ropes. The motion of the ride both hurt and woke him, and he regained full consciousness around noon. Jubal halted then and tended to his wounds, applying fresh dressings to both bullet holes. The outlaw was still bleeding internally and Jubal was torn between taking a long stop to attend to the hurts, and pushing on as fast as possible before the man died on him.

After checking the pulse and examining the hole in the raider's stomach, Jubal opted for the first choice. It would, apart from anything else, give him an opportunity to explain the situation. And a corpse was of no use at all.

He spelled it out when the one-eyed man came to.

'Hell!' The outlaw was surprised. 'You mean you shot me this way deliberate?'

Jubal nodded.

'Then you patched me together just so's I could lead you in to Klein.'

'Yeah,' said Jubal coldly. 'You got exactly two chances. The first is to stick with me and get medical attention. That way you can live a while longer if you guide me in to the hideout. The second is to die.'

'You're a hard-hearted little bastard, ain't you?' One-eye grunted. 'I always thought a sawbones took some kind of oath to help hurt people.'

'They do,' murmured Jubal, suddenly remembering his Hippocratic oath. 'Only the man who thought that up didn't think of situations like this.'

He lifted the man onto his horse and mounted up himself. Then he turned in the saddle, grinning callously.

'You better take me to Klein.'

'Suppose I don't?' One-eye asked.

Jubal pointed at the bloodstain on the outlaw's shirt. 'Lead me to Klein or die. That's doctor's orders.'

CHAPTER NINE

The one-eyed man told Jubal his life story as they rode towards Deadman Crossing. It was something to keep his body from falling off the horse, so Jubal let him ramble on, half-listening to the sad account.

His name was Jones. Arthur, his parents had called him when he was christened in Hornestown, Missouri. They had set him up in a clothing store that wasn't doing too well, so he ran away when he was seventeen. Since then he had been wandering around, picking up a living as best he could, though he wasn't too good at anything. Until he learned the art of bushwhacking and teamed up with Saul Klein.

Jubal learned a great deal about the albino from the dying man. The jayhawking part he knew about, the other pieces of information were fresh news. Klein hired out as a private gun: if someone wanted a man killed, he would handle it – if the price was right. But he maintained a base in his old Arkansas River hideout. After the War Between The States, the Union Army had tried to clean out the jayhawking stronghold. When they came, there was no one there to be cleaned out. The border raiders fled into the outlying country, lying up until the brief police action was finished. After that, by ones and twos, they came back to take up their outlaw careers where they left them. Arty Jones had returned in the late 60s. Now he wished he hadn't.

Saul Klein was a ghostly, come-and-go figure. None of his men were ever quite sure when he might show, or how long he might be gone. All they knew for certain was that they didn't cross him. That way a man got himself killed. Fast. Arty Jones was obviously as scared of offending Klein as he was of being left to die.

98

To help him make up his mind, Jubal kept reminding him of the grave extent of his wound.

It didn't take much doing. The front hole was prevented from healing over by the motion of the horse, and the exit wound was large enough to require more care than the rough stitches Jubal had applied. Around both holes, the ugly marks of gangrene were beginning to show. Given a different set of circumstances Jubal would have tended to the man as best he could and rushed him to proper care. With Andy Prescott's life in the balance, he was willing to sacrifice Jones. And the outlaw knew it: he directed Jubal to the fastest trail to the hide-out.

The direct route was negated to a certain extent by Jones' wounds. It was necessary to feed the man regular shots of morphine simply to keep him in the saddle. His wounds required cleaning out and dressing at least twice a day, and even while the ugly black excrescences of the gangrene began to putrefy the edges of the wounds, Jubal had to keep him conscious and able to ride.

On the second day he used the lariat slung on Jones' saddle to lash the man in place. By the third, the outlaw was near-delirious. He babbled madly about Hornestown and the clothing store, yelling for someone called Bobby.

On the fourth day he was incapable of going any farther. Jubal dressed his wounds and revived him as best he could. The gangrene had taken a firm hold, and it was clear that Jones would be soon dead. Jubal urged him to speak.

'Cain't ride no further.' The man's voice was a husky whisper. 'Gotta rest up.'

'I know,' said Jubal evenly. 'Tell me where the hideout is and I'll do what I can.'

They were in sight now of a range of low hills, and Jubal guessed it was the saddle that contained the hideout. Arty Jones was going to die, and all that he had left to give Jubal was the exact location.

'You'll bring help?' Jones was delirious.

'Sure,' said Jubal, 'all the help you need.'

'You promise?' Jones was frightened in the last event, his boastful courage evaporating in the face of death. 'You'll go fer help?'

'Like I promised,' said Jubal, firmly, 'all the help you need.'

Jones smiled, nodding. 'Ride west from here. You'll hit a cross trail heading south down a dry wash. Foller that towards the hills an' you'll come up to the river. Turn west fer a mile or so. You'll see a cut in the rock on the far bank. A half-mile down there's a gulley reaches west. It leads to a big cleft. That's the place.'

Jubal grinned and turned to the horses. He fed the bay some oats, then stripped the saddle from Jones' mount and turned it loose. The outlaw stretched on the Kansas sand, watching him through his one good eye. When Jubal swung into the saddle, he tried to stand up. He was too weak and fell back, groaning as the shock hit his wounds.

'You ain't gonna leave me without a horse.' His voice was faint now.

'You're not riding anywhere,' answered Jubal. 'You're dying.'

'You said you'd bring help.' Jones' cry was shriller, frightened.

Jubal shook his head. 'I promised all the help you'll need.'

'So go fetch it, fer Chrissake's.' The outlaw coughed blood as he lifted up on weak elbows. 'Don't leave me here to die.'

'There's nothing anyone can do for you,' said Jubal calmly. 'You're dying. All the help you need is prayer.'

'You bastard! Rot in hell!' Jones tried to stand up again and fell back with blood coming out of his mouth and stomach. 'You promised.'

'Pray,' said Jubal, and rode west.

By the time he reached the wash there was a spiralling column of buzzards coming down from the sky. Their dirty black wings stretched wide as they rode the air currents in lazy anticipation of the meal. When he reached the river, the birds were no longer in sight and he figured they were all on the ground, eating. He wondered if Jones was dead yet.

The Arkansas was wide and sluggish, and he forded the water easily, fetching up on the opposite bank with no sign of being spotted. He could see the cut, like a knife slash in the solid rock a few hundred yards from his position. The hills lifted up from the south bank like flat stone monuments, shutting off every approach bar the occasional clefts leading towards the south. The one Jones had described was no more than five yards wide, a narrow, sheer-walled cut with a menacing, black mouth.

Jubal walked the bay horse towards it.

He halted at the entrance and dismounted. There was no sign of guards, so he ground-hitched the horse and checked his guns over. The Spencer carried a full load, and the Colt was riding on the empty chamber with five shells snug in the cylinder. Jubal poured half the contents of a carton of .30 cartridges into his left-hand pocket, and filled the other with .45s for the handgun. He untied the two sacks from the saddle and stashed them behind a fallen rock: he might need to ride fast and want an unencumbered mount. Then he climbed into the saddle and moved cautiously down the cleft.

It was close to sunset and the gap between the rocks was shading fast into total darkness. The sound of the horse's hooves was unpleasantly loud, but there didn't appear to be anyone to hear it. At least not until he reached the westwards-facing gulley.

Then a man came out from behind a boulder with a Winchester levelled on Jubal's back.

'You gone far enuff. Rein in.'

Jubal did as he was told, bringing the bay horse to an abrupt halt. He was holding the Spencer across the saddle horn with a shell in the breech and his thumb over the curve of the hammer. He pulled the hammer all the way back as he powered backwards over the bay's haunches.

The sudden move took the guard by surprise, and his first shot blasted wild over Jubal's head. He levered the Winchester for a second shot. But it never came: Jubal's bullet was too fast. The small man in the grey suit came over the horse's withers in a tumbling dive that landed him close to the guard. As he heard the Winchester blast over his head, he rolled onto his knees, triggering the Spencer. The .30 calibre bullet hit the man directly above his belt buckle. The second shot caught him as he doubled over, exploding the apex of his skull. Jubal kept rolling, conscious of two more carbines opening up from the rocks facing him. He felt bullets plough sand around him, then he was behind the sheltering boulder.

The dead guard was sprawled across the entrance track, blood puddling around his shattered cranium. Slugs ricochetted off the stone and the bay horse snorted, digging in its heels as it went off up the gulley at a fast run.

Jubal crouched behind the rock, watching the muzzle flashes from across the ravine. There were two men there, though more would be on the way as the sounds of gunfire echoed up the canyon.

Jubal didn't plan to wait for them.

He saw a track leading up the rock face and headed for it in a bent-over run. In the waning light his grey suit was hard to spot against the rock, and he reached a ledge higher up while the Winchesters were still chipping fragments off the boulder behind the dead guard. From there he had a clear field of fire. One man was positioned on the same level, crouched down on a narrow shelf as he angled his carbine into the gulley; the other was lower down, sheltered behind a big stone. Jubal raked the ledge with fire. The light was fading too fast to give him a clear view, so he concentrated on spacing his shots along the length of the shelf. It took four before he heard the scream and the thud of a falling body. Then he angled the Spencer downwards, probing for the second man.

The guard saw his companion tumble downwards and panicked. He stood up, levering the Winchester in a wild burst of gunfire that did nothing to Jubal, but a whole lot of damage to the cliff. Jubal rose on one knee, sighting carefully. He fired once and heard the bullet hit with the soggy *thunk* that indicates a body wound.

The guard yelled and staggered into full sight. He was still holding the carbine, but the muzzle dragged through the sand and his left hand was pressed tight over his stomach. He walked out into the centre of the gulley and dropped the Winchester. Then he pressed both hands over his belly and fell down.

Jubal grinned tightly and began to reload the Spencer. He could hear hoofbeats from up the cleft and he wanted to gain height before reinforcements arrived.

He rammed a full load into the magazine and began to climb the rock. The trail was narrow and steep, but it went all the way to the top, and he made it before the horsemen found the bodies. By then the moon was up, filling the gulley with a pale wash of cold light. Jubal bellied down on the rim, watching. He counted seven riders, and guessed that as many again had stayed farther up the ravine. They checked the corpses and then began to look around. A fan of gunmen spread out, casting among the rocks for the killer. Two started up the trail, but then thought better of it and went back to their horses. Jubal smiled savagely and began to work his way along the ridge.

The hills followed the line of the river, splitting up into a series of deep clefts that radiated out from the big, west-headed ravine. He spotted numerous caves, but none showed any sign of being used. He moved on, darting amongst the broken rock that topped the ridge faster than was safe, though he remained careful not to dislodge stones into the chasm below.

It took him the better part of an hour, but then he saw a glow reflecting off the cliffs, and moved towards it. When he got to the edge, he was looking down into a wide canyon sprinkled with fires.

The hollow reached sideways off the big gulley, spreading out from a bottle-neck entrance into a bowl several hundred yards across. The walls went down like sheer glass, and huge caves gaped in the moonlight, the fires showing the men seated around the entrances. To one side of the box canyon a spring fed water to a small freshet that curved around the rock before disappearing off to the east.

Jubal knew that he had found Deadman Crossing.

He stretched flat on the rimrock, peering down. The canyon held close on twenty horses, his own bay amongst them. There were three big central fires giving off enough light for him to count eleven men. Close by the largest blaze was a man dressed all in black. Jubal recognized Saul Klein.

He looked around, but there was no sign of Andy. Only Senator Brady. The politician was spread-eagled in the centre of the canyon, his wrists and ankles lashed tight to crude pegs hammered firm into the ground. Someone had thrown a blanket over his body, but even in the moon's dim light, Jubal could see the hollows of his eyes and the old bloodstains on his face. His luxuriant white hair was dirty, matted around his temples, and he looked half-way starved.

Jubal forgot about him as he sought a route down into the stronghold.

It was close on dawn before he decided there was no way down and found a place to sleep. By then the fires were going out in the canyon and most of the outlaws had given up the search for the mysterious rifleman. Jubal had watched Klein organize search-parties after the first bunch of riders came back, and several times huddled behind sheltering rocks, or crouched in over-tight clefts, as armed men patrolled the rimrock. No one spotted him and he enjoyed the feeling of making them nervy as he listened to their shouted conversations from the tenuous safety of his hiding places.

With no quarry in sight, the outlaws returned to a defensive position in the canyon, settling down to an unrestful night. Klein posted guards around the entrance, and more along the gulley, then retreated to the largest of the caves. Jubal waited until the canyon was still, then located a deep split in the rimrock and found a rocky shelf wide enough to sleep on without rolling off. It was uncomfortable, and he slept only fitfully, but his side was hurting still and he knew he had to rest if he was to get Andy out safe.

Morning dawned damp and sunny, spreading light over the dewfall coating Jubal's clothes. He stretched, rising warily out of the cleft, holding the Spencer in stiff arms. There was no one in sight, the rimrock was empty of anything but the turkey buzzard casting speculative eyes over his supine body. The ugly bird spread its wings when he stood up, flapping madly in a desperate attempt to gain height, and launched itself over the edge of the canyon with a raucous cackle.

Jubal followed its flight on his belly, crawling over to watch the bird spiral down before it caught the updraft from the hollow and began to climb.

The bird lifted on the up-going air currents, but Jubal's gaze remained fixed on the ground below. Ives Brady was still stretched out between the pegs and some of the fires were still smouldering. Outlaws were emerging from their rocky sleeping quarters, and from the big cave came Saul Klein. He was dressed in the black suit Jubal remembered, but now he was dragging something behind him.

The something was Andy Prescott.

CHAPTER TEN

With daylight came fresh search-parties, scouring the rocks for sign of the mysterious attacker. Jubal stayed ahead of them, using the broken ground to keep out of sight. It was a wasted day that brought him no closer to freeing Andy, though by the end of it he was familiar with the terrain around the canyon. The searchers found nothing and gave up towards sunset. That left Jubal in the same position as the first night. But hungrier. He consoled himself with the thought that now he had a better idea of the canyon's layout. Klein occupied the largest cave, a vault-like hole in the rock face with a permanent fire lighting up the open ground at the front. Andy was kept under constant surveillance, and at night shepherded back into the cave. The fire negated any chance of approaching the cave unseen, and the guards posted around the entrance to the canyon meant getting in was nigh-on impossible.

Jubal hunkered down for a second cold and lonely night with his belly rumbling and his ribs aching.

In the morning he reached a decision. A plan of attack had formed in his mind during the long hours of the night and he knew that he must put it into operation soon or be too weak to carry it out successfully.

The outlaws had given up their searching, though extra guards remained posted around the canyon's approach paths. Two men with rifles and side guns barred the immediate entrance to the canyon. Up the gulley, three new men had replaced the ones Jubal had killed. One was stationed amongst the fallen rock alongside the trail; another in a split directly opposite, but ten feet up the cliff; the third was on the ledge, some thirty feet off the ground and several yards down the gulley in the direction of the hidden canyon. They were replaced at four-hourly intervals.

It was odd that no look-outs were posted on the rimrock, but Jubal guessed the outlaws felt secure enough in their stronghold to ignore the possibility of attack from above. He waited until the sun was down below the cliff's edge, and shadows dusted the gulley before making his move.

The first night guards were posted, and one had a small fire going, frying bacon behind the cover of a concealing boulder. The others were crouched watching, waiting for the sizzling strips of fatty pork to be brought up to them.

It was time for Jubal's first move.

He came down off the rock like a stalking cougar, his steps delicate and silent as he moved through the shadows. He reached the ground unseen and drifted wraith-like through the rocks. The guard was squatting over the fire, his Winchester propped against a boulder close beside his left arm. He was holding a fry-pan in his left hand while he used his right to turn the bacon. He never heard the stealthy approach of the small man in the grubby grey suit.

Jubal was carrying the Spencer in a right-handed grip, and as he came up behind the guard he swung the rifle across to cover the man's throat. The barrel pressed against his windpipe, and Jubal took the end in his left hand. In the same movement he jammed a knee hard against the guard's spine, dragging him back from the fire. The attack was sudden enough that the outlaw was shifting backwards before he could reach the Winchester, his hands coming up to claw at the metal rod cutting his mouth off from his lungs. He started to reach for the revolver at his side, and Jubal twisted the rifle, turning the man onto his face. He kept up the pressure on the throat as he swung his legs to straddle the man, tensing his legs tight down the body so that the handgun was out of reach.

Then he began to haul the Spencer upwards.

The outlaw's head came with it, arching back as inexorable pressure shuttered his breathing apparatus and curved his spine up and back. His hands struggled madly to get a grip on the barrel, but it was sunk into the loose flesh of his neck and he could gain no purchase. His eyes began to bulge, standing out from the sockets as his mouth opened in a soundless scream and his tongue protruded like a dog's on a hot day.

After a while his hands fell away and his shoulders slumped. Jubal felt the tension go from the body and dragged the Spencer back farther. There was a soft clicking sound and the outlaw's body shuddered. He urinated as he died. Jubal loosed his grip, letting the corpse fall onto the sand. He turned it over and unfastened the gunbelt. The man carried a knife and Jubal used it to hack the shirt away from the body. Then he crawled over to the fire.

The night was very still, the silence broken only by the crackling of the bacon frying in the pan. Jubal grinned and set to work.

He cut the shirt into patches that he soaked in the hot grease from the fry-pan. Then he unloaded the gunbelt and began, methodically, to remove the lead slugs from each cartridge. He poured the powder over six small squares of greasy cloth, piling black mounds of the explosive inches high. Then he gathered up the corners of each bundle and knotted them together, drawing the cloth as tight around the combustible loads as was possible. He sprinkled more gunpowder over the sticky exteriors of the packages and set them carefully aside, well away from the fire.

The dead outlaw had worn a tall, Texan-style hat. Jubal put it on, setting the brim firmly over his close-cropped black hair. There were three tin plates beside the fire and he filled two with bacon. Hurriedly, ignoring the heat, he wolfed several slices himself, then stood up, holding two plates in his left hand. He kept the Spencer in his right.

Crossing the trail towards the cleft, he tried to recall how the dead man had moved, wondering what his voice had sounded like. When the second guard called a soft enquiry, he faked a cough, mumbling something about the food being ready.

'Pass it up.'

The man stayed on his vantage point, and Jubal cursed his

watchfulness. He had to set the Spencer down to clamber over the rocks high enough to pass the plate up. He reached the ledge and set the bacon down where the man would have to reach out for it, keeping the brim of the stetson low over his face.

When the guard's arm came out to take the plate, Jubal grabbed it. As his fingers closed around the outthrust wrist, he jumped back off the rocks, dragging the outlaw with him. The man yelped once, dropping his carbine as he pitched headlong from the cleft. He hit the rocks below face-down with a sickening thud. Jubal made sure of him by the simple expedient of dropping onto his body. He felt his knees smash against bone that broke with a sharp *clicking* sound, and drove his spread palms hard onto the back of the skull. The outlaw's head smashed forcibly against the rocks, and Jubal felt a hot wetness drench his fingers.

He wiped his hands on the man's shirt and lifted the Spencer, waiting for the third guard to say something.

There was no sound, and he marvelled that his killing had been so silent. Still, the third man was the greatest problem. Perched thirty feet above the trail, he was likely to spot Jubal before it was possible to reach him. The solution to the problem was provided by the man himself: he was hungry, so he came down off the ledge.

He saw Jubal as he dropped to the ground, realizing in the instant that he landed that it was not his fellow guard waiting for him. He was right-handed. That was why his carbine was clutched in his left, the hand well away from the trigger. Jubal waited until he was on the floor of the gulley, then swung the Spencer in a double-handed grip. He was clutching the stock as the rifle arced round on a flat tangent that connected with the side of the guard's jaw. The barrel landed on his cheek, snapping his head to the side. The man staggered, dropping his Winchester. And Jubal hit him again. This time he rammed the muzzle of the rifle into the outlaw's midriff, and as he doubled over around the pain, Jubal snapped up his knee, driving the cap hard into the man's crotch. The outlaw tried to scream, but Jubal swung the Spencer back, the stock forward this time.

The wooden butt took the falling man along his temple. His mouth opened wider than ever, but the blow had crushed too many nerves to afford him time to cry out. He fell down, dead.

Jubal dragged his body back amongst the sheltering rocks and settled it beside the other corpse. Then he darted back to the fire and gathered up the bundles of gunpowder. He used the stetson to carry them in, cradling the Spencer under his right arm as he ran down the gulley.

He reached the entrance to the big canyon and ducked into cover. The two guards standing back-up duty were slouched against rocks to either side of the entrance. Jubal set his lethal bundle down behind a tumble of fragmented stone and worked his way forwards. The first guard never heard him. All he knew of the attack was the sudden explosion of pain preceding the descent of utter blackness.

Jubal lifted the Spencer, wiping gore from the stock, and cat-footed his way over to the other guard.

The man was too confident of his impregnability to hear Jubal's stealthy approach. He went down as swift and silent as his companion. Jubal used the rifle like a club, swinging it in a great round-arm blow that stove in the side of the outlaw's head. The man fell soundlessly, leaving the entrance to the canyon wide open.

Jubal crouched down, watching. Inside the rocky fortress there were fires burning, and he could smell food cooking. The smells made him hungry. He stripped both guards of their gunbelts, draping the leather over his left shoulder. Then he moved into the canyon.

He hugged the unlit side, skirting wide around the central fires, careful to avoid attention. Ives Brady was still pegged out at the centre of the hollow, though now there were two of Klein's men crouched beside him. One was feeding the Senator strips of cooked meat, while the other poked him with a knife. The politician appeared to be torn between satisfying his hunger and objecting to the pricks. As Jubal watched, hunger got the better of him and he ignored the darting knife strokes, snatching avidly the dangling meat. Both outlaws laughed as the white-maned head lunged towards the proffered food, the one withdrawing the meat while the other stuck the blade deep into Brady's leg.

Jubal looked away towards the corral. The fate of the jay-hawking Senator was no concern of his. He wanted to get Andy out: if Brady died, that was his problem.

He bellied through the shadows at the cliff's foot and reached the corral without being spotted. It was a rough wooden affair composed of uprights and cross-poles of slender branches, little more than a token barrier. Inside, the horses milled nervously as he crawled amongst them. He found a row of saddles hung on the fence and located his own. The medical bag was still in place, and he lifted it with the saddle. The bay horse recognized him and snickered a soft greeting as he draped the heavy western saddle across its back. It had been fed well since capture, and Jubal guessed it was one of the fastest animals in the stockade. He cinched the saddle tight and slid the Spencer into the scabbard. Then he went back to the other saddles. There was a switchblade knife in one, and he used it to cut halfway through the girth straps of each saddle. After that he cut lengths of rope from a lariat and used them to tie the bundles of grease-soaked explosive across the shoulders of the bay horse.

All except one.

That he kept in his hand. Mounting the bay, he fumbled matches from a vest pocket and lit a cheroot. He steered the bay over to the rear of the corral and puffed the cheroot into glowing life. Then he set the tip to the longest piece of cloth hanging from the bundle in his hand. The gunpowder coated over the bacon fat sparked into instantaneous life and Jubal tossed it across the corral.

As it landed, the flames wrapping the cloth ignited the gunpowder. The explosion was more flash than fury, but the wave of heat and the sudden flare spooked the horses, already made nervous by Jubal's presence. They screamed shrilly, shying away from the explosion. Panic gripped them and they began to charge around the flimsy corral. One big roan stallion hit the fence and rammed through the thin wood, plunging out in a welter of flailing legs and snorting, widespread nostrils. The others followed him, plunging madly away from the fire, straight across the canyon.

Jubal hung low along the bay horse's back, heading after the stampede. The charging ponies took the outlaws by surprise, careening wild down the canyon, bowling men over as they tried to halt the mad rush.

Jubal followed them on the bay, staying at the centre of the charge. As he went by one of the fires, he swung a gunbelt from his shoulder, tossing it into the flames. He did the same as he went past the next blaze. Before he reached the entrance of the canyon, he could hear the crackle of exploding cartridges adding to the confusion of the stampede.

He reached the entrance and hauled the bay to an abrupt halt. Powering from the saddle, he dragged the animal over to the rocks and unshipped the Spencer. Then he settled down to a one-man siege.

Within the canyon men were chasing shadows as furiously as they pursued their scattering horses. Klein came out of his cave with the big Smith & Wesson revolver cocked and ready, but he couldn't see anyone to fire at. The cartridge belts were exploding noisily, spraying random shots across the open ground. The staccato detonations sounded like several people were firing into the canyon and the outlaws, confused by the sporadic explosions, began firing back. They succeeded only in hitting one another and Jubal smiled coldly as he watched three of them go down with wild-fired shots in them. Still grinning, he touched the cheroot to another bundle of gunpowder. It burst into immediate flame, and Jubal's hand was burned as he tossed it high across the clearing. The flight fanned the flames into bright life, and the powder exploded in mid-air. The effect was of an incendiary shell. A spreading corona of fire flashed with a sharp bang, illuminating the confusion. Two men were directly beneath the fireball, and they began to scream as flame engulfed them.

Jubal sighted fast and shot them while they were still yelling.

He tossed a second bomb into the nearest fire and moved back to the bay horse. The gunpowder scattered the burning timber when it went off, spreading flames and chaos amongst the panicking men. Jubal swung into the saddle and took off down the canyon.

Three outlaws had managed to catch horses, but when they got saddles on the animals, they tumbled off as the severed straps parted under their weight. Jubal reached the trail up to the rimrock without hindrance. There, he left the bay ground-hitched and began to climb the narrow trail. He raced back towards the canyon, listening to the shouting that echoed from below.

Klein was rallying his men, yelling for them to fall back on the big cave. Only eight were left alive to hear him. Jubal made that seven with a snap shot off the cliff's edge. The .30 calibre bullet went through a man's knee, dropping him like a pole-axed steer. He screamed, dragging his shattered leg behind him as he clawed his way towards the cave. Jubal aimed the Spencer with automatic precision, putting the second slug through the outlaw's head.

Then the rifle was empty and Jubal had to reload. In the canyon, the gunbelts had stopped exploding, though scattered fires burned all around. It was full dark by now, and the fires were the only illumination. Klein took advantage of the gloom to get across to Brady. The politician was still spread-eagled on the ground, one hand bloodied where a stampeding horse had crushed the bones. Working fast, the albino cut Brady loose and dragged him upright. He hooked an arm around the Senator's chest, holding the half-conscious man like a human shield. His free hand held the pistol, and he turned the muzzle in on Brady's head.

'Hold it!' His voice echoed harshly through the night. 'Keep firin' an' Brady's dead!'

Jubal grinned, lighting a fresh cheroot. Klein began to move back towards the cave, confident that the attack was a rescue attempt on behalf of the politician. Jubal's crude bomb took him by surprise. It arced high into the blackness above the canyon, flaming like a shooting star as it dropped towards the white-faced killer.

Ten feet above his head it exploded.

The flash lit the canyon like a beacon. For a moment, Klein stood immobile, staring up with shocked, red-rimmed eyes. The incandescence lasted only a few seconds, but chunks of burning cloth and flaring, grease-bound fireballs rained down a miniature holocaust. Klein released Brady as his coat began to burn. He slapped at the flames, triggering wild shots in the direction of the rimrock. The handgun lacked the range and the bullets fell short of Jubal's position. He could not get a clear sight of the albino gunman through the smoke, and even though he chanced three loose bullets, the killer remained unharmed.

Ives Brady was in a worse position. The main body of the explosion had flared above him, and slightly to his front. A sheet of flame washed over him, and solid hunks of burning matter plastered against his chest. They clung to the material of his shirt, landed on his matted hair, burned. Brady screamed and tore loose from Klein's grip. A column of fire reached up from his torso, wreathing his contorted face in hellish light. His hair took fire, and he ran insanely across the open ground. His whole body became a mass of flame that pranced wildly around the canyon like some demented will-o'-the-wisp. Jubal could hear him screaming, see his arms flapping madly in a hopeless attempt to douse the fury that was consuming him. It was an awful spectacle.

Klein ran for cover as the macabre dance diverted Jubal's attention. Behind him, Brady cavorted desperately, his screams ringing like a banshee wail. Jubal grimaced, distaste and reluctant sympathy dragging down the corners of his mouth. He raised the Spencer to his shoulder, sighting down the barrel. He settled the upright notch of the foresight square between the vee of the rearsight. And squeezed the trigger. The bullet ended Ives Brady's suffering. It hit him clean in the centre of his forehead, killing him instantly. His wild capering stopped abruptly, and he stood for a moment with both arms flung wide, fire lifting from his scorched flesh. Then he toppled backwards. The flames rose from his corpse for long minutes, and Jubal could smell the stomach-turning odour of scorched flesh. He fought down the nausea, telling himself that Brady had got what he deserved. A career built on murder and robbery deserved a ghastly end. But it was still an ugly way to die.

Then he forced his attention back to the immediate problem of the outlaws. They were forted up inside the big cave and there appeared to be no way to flush them out. Opening fire on their position could endanger Andy's life. Leaving them still put the boy in danger.

Jubal made a fast decision, and set down the Spencer. He grabbed a handful of .45 shells from his coat pocket and set to biting the heads off. He used the loose powder to spread a two-foot long line of inflammable stuff against the edge of the cliff. Then he set unopened cartridges on top of the powder. Using more shells to lay a spark trail, he backed away from the rim. Three yards back he dropped the half-smoked cheroot into the powder trail, and ran for the down slope.

The cheroot burned slowly and he was halfway to the ground before the glowing tip reached the gunpowder. For a long moment the tobacco smouldered over the explosive. Then the powder ignited with a sibilant whooshing sound. A path of leaping flame raced along the fuse-trail, burning blue-yellow in the darkness. It leapt to the main layer of powder which ignited with a soft roaring noise. The cartridges heated up in the flames, their cardboard casings blackening as the gun-powder burned around them. A percussion cap exploded with a sharp crack, detonating the powder held tight within the cartridge housing. And the others followed. As Jubal reached the ground he could hear the shells going off.

From inside the canyon they should sound like someone was up on the rim with a working gun. At least he hoped they did.

He got to the floor and found the bay horse. The animal was nervous, fidgeting as the crackling fire continued. But it was still there where he had left it. He swung into the saddle and headed fast up the gulley. When he reached the entrance to the canyon, there was no sign of Klein taking his men out.

The reason why was obvious: someone was firing a Winchester at the rimrock and the remaining five outlaws were catching horses. They used the animals to shield their bodies as they hurried them back to the cave. Klein waited there with Andy held tight against his left side. He was shouting into the darkness and as the last of the burning shells went off, Jubal caught the words.

'The Senator's dead! You hear? Brady's dead!' The albino's voice carried a hysterical edge. 'I still got the boy though. You gonna risk the boy? Ease off, or I kill him.'

The final bullet exploded and the canyon fell silent. Klein peered into the darkness, deciding that his threat had paid off. He turned to his men.

'Bring my horse up. I'll go out first with the kid. You follow me.'

The outlaws didn't like it, but Klein's face was twisted up with fury and the gun in his hand cowed them. A man brought the black stallion over and the albino mounted bareback. He held Andy in front of him, the Smith & Wesson pressed tight to the youngster's side. He walked the horse forwards slowly, and behind him his men followed on.

Jubal let the albino go through. He stayed behind a fallen rock, the Spencer cocked and ready in his hands. Taking a shot was too risky: Klein might kill Andy before dying himself, so Jubal opted to play a waiting game. Klein was moving fast now, crouched low over the stallion's neck with Andy held tight against his chest. The others were more cautious, which proved to be a mistake.

Jubal came out from behind the rock as the first of the six came level with his position. He fired the Spencer from the hip, angling the muzzle upwards. The shot drilled a neat hole through the chest of the leading rider, but Jubal didn't wait to see him fall. He knew the bullet had found its target and was already swinging the gun to bear on the second man. He worked the lever almost faster than the chamber could take the shells. Snap down, haul up, squeeze. The Spencer roared continuous thunder, each bullet finding a mark. The outlaws, already panicked by the earlier attack, lost their heads completely. From their point of view the exit from the canyon was blocked by a solid wall of gunfire. It was inconceivable that one man could lay down so many shots that fast. They saw the muzzle flash as a single blast of light that accompanied the thunder and the whistle of lead.

The second man went down with one eye shot out. The third was trying to turn his horse when the man behind cannoned into him and they both pitched from their mounts with blood spreading across their chests. The last two fought their ponies to desperate, rearing stops that dragged the animals back on their haunches, blocking off the bullets. The shots hit one animal in its neck, the other through the chest, and the shrill keening of the wounded horses was added to the symphony of death.

Jubal dropped the Spencer and lifted the Colt. The handgun blasted a deeper note as he extended his right arm in the classic firing stance and picked off the remaining two outlaws. One he hit as the man jumped clear of his dying horse, throwing him back against the animal so that it rolled over him, muffling his final scream. The other landed on hands and knees, gaping wide-eyed at the carnage spread before him. His eyes stayed open as Jubal's bullet blew away the front of his skull and he slumped face-down in the sand.

The whole incident had taken no more than three minutes. Jubal used two more to shoot the wounded horses and check over the bodies. The outlaws were all dead, each one showing a single, lethal wound. Jubal left them where they lay and mounted the bay horse. Klein had a start of around five minutes: Jubal intended to cut it down.

He heeled the bay to a gallop, riding headlong down the gulley. Fear for Andy's safety made him careless. He should have known that a man like Saul Klein was unlikely to lose his nerve, and while keeping it would use every sneaky trick he could think of. All Jubal could see was Andy's face as the albino took him out of the canyon. It had been set firm, the blue eyes staring dead ahead almost as though the boy could see where he was going, the mouth fixed in a grim line. Andy had been putting a bold front on things, even though Jubal could guess at his fear. It was that concern that made him abandon his usual caution. And almost cost him his life.

He came fast around a long curve in the ravine and heard a shot. Pure reflex action took over as he powered from the saddle, dragging the bay's head over and down. The big horse crashed to the sand as Jubal rolled sideways with a second bullet splintering stone close above his head.

'Hold back or the kid's dead!' Klein's voice rang loud through the gulley.

Jubal hugged ground, flattening against the sand in a pretence of death. He trusted to Klein's mistaken belief in a large posse to hurry the man on his way without checking over the 'corpse'. After a while, he heard the sound of a horse moving out.

'The rest o' you stay back,' yelled Klein. 'I got a gun on the boy an' I'll kill him if you try anything. Stay back an' he might live. That's my only offer.'

Jubal heard the bravado in the albino's voice and looked off down the lightening trail. The man was out of sight as he climbed to his feet, dusting himself down.

'That's one offer I have to refuse,' he grunted.

CHAPTER ELEVEN

Saul Klein rode west and south, making for the Oklahoma Territory. He knew people there who would hide the boy — for a share in the ransom money. It never occurred to the gunman to doubt his chances of getting away safely, even though he was pretty sure his gang was finished.

The attack on the hideout had taken him by surprise. He had counted on trouble after taking Brady prisoner, but had figured it to come days later in the form of a big posse. The citizens of Angel lacked the spine to take off after him so fast, yet no large body of men had entered the rocks. The devastating fury of the raid suggested a determined rescue party; the ruthless shooting of the politician didn't tie in. Klein was irritated: he didn't like problems of that nature. But if the rescuers weren't there for the Senator, then they must have come for the boy. He mulled it over as he followed the river. It was always possible Agnew had sent bounty hunters after him, or maybe the dead Pinkerton had been waiting for reinforcements.

The albino shrugged: the Pinkerton Agency already had a warrant on him for a killing in Arkansas, one more wouldn't stretch his neck any farther. He was wanted in a whole lot of places. Had been for years. He smiled: thinking about his murderous career always cheered him up.

It had begun back in the '40s, in Rolla, Missouri. The other kids had always taunted him because of his white skin and hair, the pink eyes. It meant that he learned to use his fists and feet early on, learning the hard way to beat kids a deal bigger than him. At the age of nine he left a fourteen-year-old boy stretched in the dust of the schoolyard with blood coming from his split skull. They found young Saul still clutching the jagged stone, carefully cleaning the blood from the shard edge.

When the same thing happened to three more boys, his father had upped stakes and moved the family to Kansas City. It was an unfortunate move: the man got shot dead by a drunken rail ganger two days after reaching the town. Saul didn't care particularly and his mother remarried fast enough that they never got short of money.

Jared Klein was a Mormon. He was a kind enough man, but a firm believer in discipline: Saul learned to hate him, and the heavy leather belt he wore. Feelings against the Mormons ran high in Missouri and Jared decided to sell out his hardware store and head for Brigham Young's promised land in the Utah Territory. By then, Saul had practised enough with his stepfather's trade guns to be proficient. He was fifteen when the wagons quit Kansas City on the long road west. Their plan was to follow the Smoky Hill River west through Kansas into Colorado, then they would fork north to pick up the Central Overland Trail where it curved along the Platte River into Wyoming before dropping down past Fort Bridger to Salt Lake City. Saul only got as far as Angel. There, Jared unbuckled his big leather belt one time too many. The white-haired boy had taken a hog-leg pistol and beaten the Mormon half-dead. Jared made the rest of the trip stretched out on a mattress in the back of his wagon. Saul had run off and drifted around the Kansas territory until he met up with Ives Brady and Vance Graves.

The border troubles had seemed like a godsend to the three young men. They were all hungry for excitement and anxious to get rich. Jayhawking seemed to solve both wants. When his former friends left him for dead, Klein had vowed to pay them back. He had tried when he lead the army to the Deadman Crossing hideout, but that counter-betrayal hadn't worked and he was forced to wait. A deal of the waiting was done in the Cavalry through the long years of the Civil War. When the conflict ended, Klein found himself in Nebraska with no particular place to go. He drifted down through Colorado into Arizona, and found employment. The Butterfield Mail was having trouble with road agents and needed men who could use a gun for more than hammering nails. Klein got three dollars a day and whatever reward money was posted on the bodies he brought in. In two months he made a clear thousand dollars and the beginning of his reputation. When the mail routes were safe and life got boring again, he drifted up to Nevada. In Carson City a mine owner hired him to put a stop on the robberies of ore shipments. Klein learned a few names and left a trail of corpses behind him. The robberies stopped. After that he wandered around California for a while, using his lethal talents on the Barbary Coast.

Then he took it into his head to see his mother again.

By then she scarcely recognized him. He was topping six feet and had taken to wearing black, as though deliberately contrasting his albinoism with the darkness of his clothes. He wore a Smith & Wesson Russian tied down on his right hip, and what had been a youthful lust for excitement had turned to a cold contempt for human life. Martha Klein saw it in her son's red eyes and took to praying for him. Jared was less charitable. Reluctantly, thinking of his wife, he invited Saul to stay. By then he had a younger women, a buxom Mormon girl who took a shine to Saul, entranced by his strange appearance and contained deadliness.

Jared found them in bed one sunny August afternoon and reached for the shotgun he kept above the fireplace. Klein strangled the old man before he could use the gun. Then – to be on the safe side – he strangled the girl too. He carried her body into the master bedroom and dragged his stepfather in. He fired one barrel of the scattergun into the girl's neck, obliterating the fingermarks bruising her flesh. The other barrel he fired into his stepfather's mouth. Then he ran from the house yelling about suicide.

No one really believed the story, but there was no proof with which to confront the murderer, so the Mormons let him stay. He settled his mother's affairs and deposited two thousand dollars in her name. It was most of his bounty money, but he figured he could make it up again and having a base in Salt Lake City was potentially useful. He even bought himself a plot in the cemetery and afterwards, if anyone asked where he came from, he told them: 'Salt Lake City.'

He stuck around long enough to see his mother safe, then moved off eastwards. The Dakota Territory was crawling with Indians so he moved on to Minnesota and Wisconsin. Three killings – and a thousand dollars – later, he moved on to Iowa. By the time he reached Illinois he had made up his two thousand grubstake. The Mississippi took him south to New Orleans, where he made more money. Louisiana grew too hot and he drifted over into Texas. Guns commanded premium prices along the Brazos and Klein enhanced his reputation amongst the Texan cattle barons. Oklahoma proved equally fertile country for a good gunhand, and he whiled away the better part of a year there. He was into his thirties before he saw Kansas again. It hadn't changed much, except the towns he remembered were a building or two bigger and Vance Graves was sheriff of Angel.

The news didn't surprise Klein. By then there was very little that did. He thought about killing Vance, but put it off until he could find out about Ives. The news came after three months of profitable robbery. The Deadman Crossing canyon was headquarters of a cut-throat gang that accepted Saul Klein as leader after he shot an outlaw called Curly Rhodes who thought he was the boss. Klein directed operations in a way that made everyone richer: being a hired assassin allowed him an insight into the affairs of the wealthy that was denied his humbler companions. A banker in Nashville, Tennessee, told him about Senator Ives Brady. A Missouri rancher told him about the Senator's proposed visit to Kansas. A businessman in Chicago gave him the dates.

And Saul Klein decided to settle the old scores.

Now they were settled. He had enjoyed killing Vance. The old jayhawker had let himself grow too fat and complacent on stolen money. Seeing him suffer had been the most fun Klein had had in a long time. It was a pity Ives had died under someone else's gun, but the days preceding his death had been long and filled with pain. He had been hurting when he died and that gave Klein a warm feeling in the pit of his stomach. The only irritation was not knowing who had fired the shot. He had seen one man coming after him down the gulley and figured the rider to be a headstrong leader of the posse. The rapid fire from the rim of the canyon, coming so fast after the initial raid, suggested a bunch of skilled marksmen. The shots that had killed the men following him out must have come from at least three hidden rifles. Klein hoped the attackers would stay around the canyon long enough to give him a clear lead.

He pushed the black stallion on at a killing pace, holding the blind boy like a shield across his chest.

It was odd, but he had almost grown to like the boy while holding him prisoner. He had a will of his own and enough courage for a full-grown man and, in a warped kind of a way, his lost sight made him kin to Klein. They both suffered a physical affliction that set them apart from other people. Klein wouldn't hesitate to kill the boy if he had to, but he vaguely hoped it wouldn't come to that. Apart from anything else, the kid represented a fat chunk of Ben Agnew's money that would fit nicely in Klein's pocket.

He rode on into the brightening morning, wondering where he could find a saddle.

Close on noon a lonely homestead offered the answer. It was built into a bluff south of the Arkansas, a low-roofed soddy with a small corral flanking the shack and hogs rooting dirt in front. Klein rode up to it and dismounted. He lifted Andy down and drew his gun.

'You won't make it.' The words surprised him. They were the first the boy had spoken since riding out of the canyon. 'That was Jubal Cade back there. He's coming after me. He's gonna get you. It's like my paw used to say: when it's got yore name on it, you ain't gonna get away.'

'Yore paw talked too much,' grunted Klein. 'Hold the horse an' keep yore mouth shut.'

He turned towards the soddy. So far there was no sign of life except for the hogs and two horses shuffling around the corral. He eased his coat back from the butt of the Smith &

Wesson and walked up to the door. It opened a fraction as he reached the stoop and a rifle poked out. It was an old single-shot Henry and from the way it inched through the crack, Klein guessed it was held by a woman.

'Howdy.' He made his voice sound friendly. 'Had a little trouble with road agents. Me an' the boy need some water an' a saddle if you got one to sell.'

The rifle stayed pointed at his stomach, but his words had given him time to get close up to the door. He waited on the porch, calculating his chances.

'There's water in the river, mister.' The answer was given in a feminine tone. 'An' we ain't got no saddle to spare. Ride on afore my man comes back.'

Klein smiled: the information was useful.

'The boy needs food, ma'am. He's tuckered out. You surely got a plate o' somethin' to spare for him.'

For a moment, the rifle muzzle dropped as the woman behind the door peered through to look at Andy. The blind boy was standing beside the stallion, his head cocked to one side as he listened to the conversation.

Abruptly, he shouted. 'Kill him, ma'am! He's an outlaw!'

Klein swore, snaking forward as the barrel of the Henry lifted in his direction. He got his left hand around it, turning it off to the side as the bullet blasted out. The slug hit a hog that squealed and took off across the river. Klein lifted the S&W in one smooth movement triggering a shot through the thin woodwork of the soddy's door. There was a scream from inside and the sound of a body falling. Klein dragged the rifle through and fired a second shot to be safe. He angled the pistol downwards, firing through the opening. Then he put his shoulder to the wood, breaking the length of rope that held it partway closed, and stepped inside.

The woman was sprawled on the plank floor. The front of her cheap gingham dress was staining red where the first bullet had hit her, and the lower part of her face was a bloody mess where the second had blown her jaw away. She was dead.

'Hey, kid.' Klein looked towards Andy. 'You shoulda kept yore mouth shut. I had to kill thanks to you.'

He grinned nastily as he watched a tear gather in the corner of Andy's sightless eye. It rolled down the youngster's dirty cheek, followed by several more as the boy realized what had happened.

'Guess you'll have that on yore conscience,' said Klein, his tone conversational. 'You thought about that?'

Andy turned his face towards the sound. His eyes were clear and blue, wet with the tears, but fixed on the gunman's face as though he could see Klein. It was, the albino realized, unnerving.

'Not my conscience,' said Andy firmly. 'Yours. You pulled the trigger. You're the one that killed her.'

Klein snarled, dragging the boy into the cabin. He shoved him to one side as he hunted out food and located two canteens. A drawer revealed a carton of .44 ammunition that would fit the Smith & Wesson, and he emptied it into his coat pocket. He stuffed meat into a flour sack, then filled the canteens at the well behind the shack. Then, dragging Andy with him, he went out to the corral. A lean-to contained a couple of worn saddles and a selection of harness in need of repair. Klein selected the better of the two rigs and put it on the black stallion. When he saw the empty rifle scabbard he cursed, regretting the loss of his Winchester. The old Henry was a poor substitute, but he loaded it anyway and shoved it into the scabbard. The two horses were sorry-looking beasts and he checked them over with an angry expression before saddling the stronger of the pair. He led the animal over to the boy and guided Andy's hands to the reins.

'Can you ride?' It was a thought that hadn't occurred to him before.

'Sure.' Andy sounded insulted. 'Just because I can't see don't mean I've forgotten everything.'

He fumbled at the stirrup, guiding his left foot into position, and – with a degree of awkwardness – got astride the pony. Klein watched him, feeling again the reluctant admiration. Just as he had come to terms with his appearance, so Andy seemed to refuse to allow his blindness to hamper him any more than was inevitable.

'I'll say this for you, kid,' he murmured. 'You got what it takes.'

Andy said nothing, just sat the horse in silence as the albino looped a rope around his ankles. When Klein was finished the rope secured Andy's legs to the saddle with a length running under the pony's belly. There was no way the boy could dismount without help. Klein used a further length of rope to fashion a lead rein, tying the free end around his own saddle horn. After that he mounted and rode away in the direction of the Cimarron.

Andy followed behind, wondering where they were headed. Klein didn't speak for the next few miles, but the boy could sense his nervousness and knew that the man was looking behind a lot.

He wondered how long it would take Jubal to catch up.

CHAPTER TWELVE

The fall had done Jubal's damaged side no good at all, and his ribs were hurting as he mounted the bay horse and started after Klein and Andy. The horse was unharmed and running it was a good way to diminish its nervousness at the rough treatment. It took off down the gulley as though it was as anxious as its rider to catch up. Jubal gave the animal its head until they broke clear of the hills. The sun was up by now and the Arkansas sparkled blue in the clear morning light. Along the bank of the river Jubal could see tracks following the water. There was a whole mess of hoofprints where riders had come into the hills, but they pointed mostly to the north and east, and dewfall was silvering the indentations with trapped moisture. The set Jubal was studying looked to be deeper than the others, as though the horse carried a heavy load. And they were dry.

Jubal followed them westwards. They ran along the bank of the river for about two miles, then turned south into open country. For an hour, they remained clear in the Kansas dirt. After that they petered out over rocky ground. When Jubal lost the trail, it appeared to be headed due south. He reined in the bay, letting the animal rest while he revised his geography. The Arkansas rose in the Sangre de Cristo range, way off in Colorado. It ran eastwards to join the Mississippi, crossing Kansas on a bisecting line. Below it ran the Cimarron, looping up out of New Mexico to hook into Kansas before dropping down into the Cherokee Outlet and the Oklahoma Territory. The Outlet bordered with Kansas, but west of the strip lay the 150-mile extension of Oklahoma, a buffer between Kansas and the northernmost spread of Texas. The tracks pointed that way, and Jubal guessed that Klein was heading for the Territory. He turned his horse south.

A while later he spotted the soddy. It was unusually still, and the door was open to let the hogs inside. The big, dirty brown pigs were rooting busily around the door. When Jubal went in he understood why.

He chased the hogs out of the cabin and closed the door. The dead woman wasn't pretty by then, but he picked up the body anyway and set it on the table at the centre of the shack. He found a cheap cotton tablecloth and spread it over the corpse, noticing the ransacked cupboards. He was turning to leave when he heard the hoofbeats. Innate caution prompted him to back up behind the door, and instinct shifted his hand to the Colt under his left arm. When the door flew open, habit proved a safe thing.

The man who stepped through was young and worried. The Creedmore rifle he held out in front of him looked big and dangerous. Jubal decided against taking chances on misunderstandings. Instead, he let the man get inside the cabin, holding back against the wall as the man paused, seeing the cloth-shrouded figure of his wife for the first time. Frontier training showed in his movements as he went down on one knee with the rifle shifting round to cover the interior of the cabin.

He saw Jubal and began to tighten his finger on the Creedmore's trigger. At that kind of range the heavy-calibre rifle could have blown Jubal out through the soddy's wall, but the man saw the Colt before he closed in the last fraction of trigger slack.

'Why?' His voice was pain and disbelief intermingled. 'Why'd you kill her?'

'I didn't.' Jubal stood ready to fire the Colt if he had to. He hoped it wouldn't come to that. 'I found her on the floor. I was just laying her out.'

'Yeah.' The homesteader's voice was bitter. 'You're a passin' undertaker lookin' fer business. Tell the truth before I let you have it.'

Jubal held the Colt steady on the man's chest. 'I didn't kill her. I think I know who did.'

128

'So do I,' muttered the man. And fired the rifle.

Long months of living close to death had taught Jubal Cade to sum up his opponents in seconds. Professional guns remained calm, impassive right up to the instant of firing. Their eyes betrayed nothing of their intentions, and when they were ready to shoot the only indication was a tightening of their gunhand, an almost imperceptible movement of the trigger finger. Men unused to killing showed it in their eyes. Facial muscles grew tense as they prepared themselves to take a life. Mostly, their eyes narrowed down as they concentrated on the target, and often their mouths thinned out in anticipation of the blast.

The young homesteader showed all the latter signs. Jubal saw them, and knew exactly when the shot was coming. He powered sideways as it went off. Deliberately, he held back the hammer of the Colt so that he hit the floor without the pistol going off. The Creedmore's slug hit the wall behind him and went on through, the blast rocking the homsteader back on his heels. He was trying to work another shell into the breech as Jubal came up on his knees with the Peacemaker stuck out about two inches from the man's face.

'Drop it!' Jubal's voice was urgent. 'I'll kill you if I have to.'

The homesteader let the rifle drop to the floor.

'Why not?' His voice was lost, despairing. 'I got nuthin' to live for any more.'

Jubal felt the man's pain. 'I lost my own wife. It hurts, but it doesn't finish you. Bury her and go on.'

The man looked up. His eyes were thick with tears, but something akin to hope showed in them. He stared at Jubal as though he had trouble assimilating the words.

'You didn't kill her?'

Jubal shook his head: 'No.'

'Then who did? The homesteader glanced round at the shrouded figure. 'Why?'

'I think it was a man callen Klein,' answered Jubal. 'A hired gun. I've been chasing him. He came out of a place called Deadman Crossing riding bareback. I reckon he needed saddles and a fresh mount: he had someone with him.'

'I left two ponies in the corral,' said the homesteader. 'Could be he took one. There was saddles too.'

Suddenly, he was trusting Jubal. It might have been that the Colt had not been used, or the urgency of Jubal's voice, but he now trusted the dirty man in the grey suit.

'Let's go check.'

Jubal lowered the Colt's hammer and dropped the gun into the shoulder holster. He noticed that the homesteader left the rifle on the floor and walked through the door as though he was no longer worried about a bullet. The exact reasons for the abrupt change in attitude didn't worry him: finding Klein's trail was the important thing.

Both the homesteader's spare saddles were gone, and one of his horses. After a while, he realized that his second rifle was missing too. Jubal worked it out fast. Klein must have stopped at the cabin to pick up a horse for Andy. The woman had tried to stop him and died for her troubles: Saul Klein wouldn't hesitate to shoot a female if she got in his way. He left the homesteader mourning his lost wife and set off south-wards. There was a whole passel of tracks leading that way, and somewhere down the line, Andy Prescott was waiting to be rescued.

Exactly where was a thing Jubal Cade intended to find out. Soon.

He rode away from the homestead with his gaze fixed on the Kansas dirt. There were two sets of tracks now. One set was wide and deep, looking to be a long-legged horse carrying a full-grown man; the other was shorter and less deep: the kind of trail a farm horse would make if it was ridden by a light-weight. He followed them southwards through the day, and around mid-afternoon came to a place where they stopped. There was sign of two people dismounting and a scattering of discarded food, as though they had eaten in a hurry too urgent to permit much time for chewing.

The tracks went to the south. Jubal followed them.

He followed them until it got too dark to see any more and the far reaches of the flatlands were shrouded in blackness. The moon was thinning out and heavy clouds scudded like runaway smoke across the sky. Jubal found a dry wash and made camp. He didn't think Klein would be laying for him, so he got a fire going and prepared a meal. It was the first real food he had eaten in days, and his stomach protested at the sudden influx. When he was finished he stripped down to the waist, shivering as the prairie cold hit him, and removed the bandages covering his side. The dressings were long over-due for changing, and he used the contents of his medical bag to cleanse the wounds. They were mostly healed, though his ribs showed thin against his flesh, and where Klein's bullet had broken them two raised lumps indicated the knitting of the bones. He wound fresh bandages around his body with diffi-culty and dug a clean shirt from his saddlebag.

The coffee pot was steaming and he poured a mug of the bitter liquid, lacing it with whiskey. The night was very cold and he was hurting; the whiskey eased the aches and he sipped it gratefully, leaning back on his saddle. Above him, the sky was a seething mass of cloud that blocked out the stars, threatening rain.

It started up halfway through the following morning. Jubal felt a whole lot better for a night's solid sleep and a decent meal. He heated up the coffee pot and fried bacon as the sun tried to push its way through the gloomy sky. The bay horse was fresh and ready to go again, so he moved out while the sun was still barely over the horizon. Then the rain came.

It came with a ferocious abruptness, the only warning a great rolling peel of thunder that forked lightning down towards the ground. Immediately after, a solid sheet of water shut out the trail. Klein's tracks disappeared as though a giant hand was wiping the land clean. Jubal dragged his slicker around his shoulders, moving on with water spilling off the brim of his derby. It washed down his face, driving into his eyes as the wind got up and lashed at the lonely rider. The world was shut out behind a curtain of grey water, and the horse's steps sounded like soggy mops striking a waterlogged floor. It stayed that way for most of the day, so that the only indication of sunset was a further darkening of a sky already black.

Jubal was riding on pure guesswork. He had no means of knowing where Klein might have gone with Andy, nor whether he might have passed them in the rain. He figured, though, that the albino would push on southwards, trying to put distance between himself and Deadman Crossing.

Following through the storm-filled night was a loser's game, so he began to look for some kind of dry camp. Nothing showed as he reached the Cimarron, and he skirted the bank in search of a ford. The river was high, the storm lashing its surface to a foaming grey turbulence. Jubal found what looked to be a likely place to cross and fought the bay horse into the river. He was soaked all the way through when they climbed out on the far bank, and his teeth were starting in to chattering. There was no sign of any decent place to dry out. Jubal wished he had a waterproof tent with him.

Then a light showed through the sleeting downfall. He steered towards the glow. He was six feet away before anyone saw him, the Spencer cocked in his hands – though he wasn't sure it would fire after the Cimarron crossing.

The light came from a lantern hung under the tailgate of a wagon, and as Jubal peered through the rain he made out the shapes of three Conestogas drawn up in a rough triangle.

'Hold it right there!'

The words carried an implicit threat. The threat was backed up with a bullet. The bullet spun raindrops into Jubal's face as it whistled past his head. The discharge of the carbine was lost in the roaring murmur of the rain.

'Next one drops you!'

Jubal heard the *click* of the lever action as the rain swirled clear for a moment, and shouted: 'Go easy! I'm not looking for a fight. Just someplace dry.'

'That's what the other one said.' A second voice shouted

through the rain. 'You want to come in, you do it with yore hands held high where we can see 'em. An' do it slow.'

Jubal dropped the Spencer's hammer and slid the rifle back into the scabbard. When he raised his arms, rain came in under the lifted sides of his stormcoat: he was too wet for it to make any difference.

'Climb down slow, mister.' The first voice sounded a little more friendly. 'An' keep yore hands in the air.'

Jubal steered the bay horse between the wagons with his knees, watching the men who showed to either side of him. They came out from behind the Conestogas with carbines aimed on his chest. He was unpleasantly conscious of the guns as he dropped from the saddle, and careful to keep both arms lifted high. One man stuck the muzzle of his Le Mat against the small of Jubal's back while the other frisked him. It was an inexpert performance that failed to locate the shoulder-holstered Colt. But they took the Spencer. Jubal waited for them to finish, using the time to study the camp.

Tarpaulins were draped from the tailgates of the wagons, so that a crude canvas verandah stretched around the triangle. Three women huddled nervously beneath one stretch, clutching frightened children to their heavily coated bosoms. A fitful cooking fire spluttered beneath a black stewpot, protected from the rain by an out-pegged reach of canvas. And a corpse was stretched under another wagon.

'Hiram got shot this morning,' said the man with the Le Mat. 'Feller rode in calling fer food. After he'd eaten he called fer a fresh horse. Said he needed it fer the kid.'

'Kid?' Jubal said. 'He had a kid with him?'

'Why, sure,' answered the pioneer, his voice curious. 'Tall little feller with starey eyes.'

'The man,' rasped Jubal, 'what was he like?'

'Pretty weird. He was dressed all in black an' his face was kinda white. Had eyes like coals. They looked to be goin' right through you. Hiram said he couldn't have a horse. Next thing we knew, Hiram was killed stone-dead. I never seen a man so fast with a handgun.'

'When did they go?' The urgency in Jubal's voice communicated to the pioneers.

'Around five.' The younger spoke, holding a wire-bound Winchester on Jubal's chest. 'He looked over the horses like he owned them. Picked out the best an' began to saddle it. Hiram took exception an' got shot. 'Fore we could do anything, there was a pistol pointed on us.'

'The boy,' grated Jubal. 'Was he all right?'

'He was well enough. His horse was played out though. That was why the feller said he wanted a remount.'

'Klein.' The words broke from Jubal's mouth like a curse.

'You know him?' The younger man looked nervous. 'How come?'

'He has something I want,' said Jubal sourly. 'Something that belongs to me. I've been chasing him through to here.'

'Anyone who knows that man ain't no friend of ours,' grunted the oldster. 'Maybe you'd best ride on.'

'After you tell me something,' said Jubal, facing the rifles. 'Where was he headed?'

'Why in the hell should we tell you?' The question was compounded of bitterness and mistrust. 'Fer all we know, you're with him.'

'Where?' Jubal asked. 'I'll kill you if you don't tell me.'

The older man snorted scornfully. 'You're one man, feller. You gonna take us both?'

Jubal nodded. 'If I must.'

'Fer Chrissakes, Josh.' The younger of the riflemen spoke through the darkness. 'If he was ridin' with Klein, he'd have tried somethin' by now. Tell him where the bastard went and let's get on our way.'

'Yeah, could be you're right, Pat.' Jubal felt the tension ease, an almost palpable feeling. 'Maybe we should.'

Pat took the initiative. Jubal felt the rifle drop away from his back and glanced around at both the men. The rain was easing off, and the lanterns showed the tired lines decorating their faces. They looked beaten and wary.

'Where did they go?'

134

'South,' grunted the one called Pat. 'Ain't nuthin' 'twixt here an' there except a ghost town called Burch. It's empty o' everythin' bar tumbleweeds an' sand.'

Jubal heard the news and fought the temptation to ride away into the night. He needed food and rest as much as the bay horse, so he accepted Josh's grudging invitation to eat. They spooned a watery stew while the old man told him about their misfortunes. Bound for California, they had missed their trail and drifted too far south; now they were just looking for somewhere to settle. Hiram had been their leader – until Saul Klein showed up and killed him. Now they weren't sure where to go. Jubal refrained from advising them, limiting his conversation to a sparse minimum. Burch was a day's ride south, a burned-out mining town that had never managed to bring in its promised payload. There was nothing there except the empty buildings: a good place for a hunted man to hole up.

Jubal found the place at sunset the next day.

He quit the bedraggled pioneers just after dawn. The rain had stopped, and the sun was lifting streamers of mist off the prairie. Josh and Pat – Jubal never learned the names of the women – were planning to head on westwards. He wished them luck and rode south. Burch was his best – his only – chance of finding Klein, so he headed for the deserted town.

Along the way, his clothes and his guns dried out. He halted around noon to check over the Spencer and the Colt. Both were in good working order, though the handgun's shoulder holster was somewhat stiffened by the soaking of the rain and the river crossing.

When he saw Burch, the sun was a big orange globe that spread light across an empty landscape. He was close to the border with Oklahoma, and the setting sun was throwing long shadows off the empty buildings. Jubal watched them from the ridge above the town. They looked lonelier than anything he had seen. The cluster of dried-out shells was situated at the centre of a deep, wide depression in the plain.

Old mineheads stood out like forsaken tombstones around the place, tracks of forgotten wagons leading in from the workings to the single street of the forgotten town. There was a two-storey hotel built on hope, and a saloon that had lost its dreams. A cobwebbed cluster of stores and a tumbledown stable finished the tragic ensemble.

The place looked as forlorn as anything he had seen, an empty reminder of human frailty.

Halfway down the single street there were two horses hitched to a part-fallen rail.

Jubal turned the bay along the ridge to come in to Burch from behind. The two horses were hitched outside the empty saloon. They looked tired, their sides were heaving and their heads hanging down. One was a tall-standing stallion, its coat black as midnight; the other was a sway-bellied cart-horse that looked like it was more used to wagon shafts than saddles. Jubal wrapped a length of bandage around the muzzle of the bay horse before he rode in, a precaution against the animal whickering a greeting to the others.

He reached the edge of the empty town and dismounted. He was at the back of the saloon, and when he tried the rear door he found it jammed. He put a trail of footprints through the gathered sand as he skirted the building. Then he worried about the noise he made ploughing through the muck gathered over the porch. He was carrying the Spencer rifle with the hammer all the way back to full-cock, and he reached the door of the saloon unseen.

Ducking low to stare under the batwings, he watched for Klein. The albino was nowhere in sight, but Jubal saw Andy Prescott sitting alone on a chair at the centre of the big, empty room. The boy lifted his head as Jubal moved back around the door. He couldn't see anything, but he gave an impression of knowing exactly what was happening. His sightless blue eyes shifted over to stare towards the lonesome street, and a soft cry burst from his lips.

'Jubal! I knew you'd come.'

Jubal started forwards, but then cold metal pressed against

his temple, and he heard a harsh, disbelieving voice close by his ear.

'I never thought to meet you again,' grated Saul Klein.

Jubal tensed, staring at Andy's empty, hopeless eyes.

'Seeing is believing,' he muttered.

CHAPTER THIRTEEN

'How'd you find me?'

Klein sounded genuinely interested, as though his professional pride was at stake.

'You left a trail,' said Jubal bitterly. 'The woman in the cabin, the man from the wagons. And you forgot something.'

'What?' Klein asked. 'I figgered the rain had washed the tracks out. I never thought anyone could follow me through that.'

'You got something I want,' answered Jubal. 'More than Agnew, more than you. You got Andy.'

The albino laughed, glancing over towards the boy. 'The kid's worth fifteen thousand dollars of Agnew's money to me. What's he worth to you?'

'Everything,' said Jubal simply. 'I'll kill you before you take him out of here.'

Klein laughed again. It was a lonely sound in the emptiness of Burch. It echoed around the wind-scoured walls of the deserted saloon, bouncing back off the peeling planks to reverberate around his tilted head. It sounded as wild as the wind, and almost as mad. Jubal watched from the chair beside Andy's. Klein hadn't bothered to tie him, just lifted the Peacemaker from the shoulder holster and tossed it off to one side of the room. It was resting on a bank of drifted sand, temptingly close; too far away to reach. The albino was holding the Smith & Wesson Russian cocked in his right hand, the matching pistol tucked into his belt. When he finished laughing, he shook his head, studying Jubal's face.

'You mean it was just you at the canyon? You did all that?'

Jubal nodded.

'Jesus Christ.' Klein sounded almost admiring. 'I thought

it was a whole goddam posse. What happened to Arty Jones an' the others?'

'I killed them,' said Jubal.

'You're a mean little fucker, ain't you?' Klein said thoughtfully. 'Near as mean as me.'

He stared hard at Jubal. The smaller man sat easily on the rickety chair, his features creasing with anger. The fury brewing up behind his eyes was the most impressive thing about him. Apart from that he was a pretty undistinguished figure. His suit was crumpled and dirty from the long ride, heavy beard stubble shaded his cheeks and his hair was growing out in straggly tufts that hung down from the brim of the grey derby. He hadn't bothered to wash in the last twelve hours, and his thinned-out face was streaked with dirt that almost hid the blue shadows under his hollow-rimmed eyes. As Klein watched, the eyes narrowed and the grubby skin drew taut across Jubal's cheek-bones. Through the dirt, a band of pale scar tissue stood out white over the bridge of his nose.

Somehow, the expression unnerved Klein. It made him feel that perhaps this crazy little guy might carry out his promise: might kill him. No matter what the cost. He didn't enjoy the feeling. He wasn't used to it.

'Let the boy go.'

Jubal's plea was direct and simple, and every ounce of feeling in his body and his soul was put into the words.

'Go to hell.' Klein's answer was equally direct.

'You'll be opening the gates,' said Jubal.

Andy Prescott shifted his head from side to side, listening hard as he worked out the exact positions of both men. Being blind for so long had taught him to use his ears better than any sighted person would: he could estimate a man's position and distance by the sound of a footfall, calculate a change of posture by the faint grinding of a heel on soft wood. He knew that Jubal was sitting about two feet to his right, that Klein was standing four feet in front of them. He could sense the tension without hearing the bitter exchange of words.

'My paw always said that when you're in need.' His sudden interruption diverted the attention of both men. 'You'd best act fast.'

Andy pitched from his chair as the sentence ended. He hurled himself straight at Saul Klein, guessing the direction from the shifting of the man's boots on the sandy floor. The move took the albino completely by surprise. He had been waiting for Jubal to take a chance; the boy's rush was a total shock. It threw his aim off so that the S&W exploded wild into the ceiling. A rusted lantern tore loose from its fitment as the .44 calibre bullet blasted through the stanchion attaching it to the roof. Then wiry arms wrapped tight around his wrists, legs drummed hard against his shins, and he grunted as sharp teeth sunk deep into his gunhand.

Jubal powered out of the chair as Andy moved. His reaction was totally instinctive, born of danger and the need to react on pure reflex in order to stay alive. He went forwards and to the side. He felt his elbow slam into Klein's knee, his shoulder smash against the albino's hip. Then he was rolling clear with sand ripping his skin as he reached for the Colt. He closed his fingers around the butt and lifted the revolver. Sand dribbled from the muzzle as he swung it round, thumbing the hammer back.

Klein was perched on one knee, his left hand balled up into a fist as he pummelled Andy's head. The boy was hanging on to the albino's right wrist like a bulldog, and Jubal could see blood pumping from the teethmarks even as he fired the Peacemaker.

It was a calculated chance. Saul Klein was unable to use his revolver while Andy clung to his hand, and he was too busy punching the boy to pull the belt gun clear. If he got a chance, he would use Andy as a shield: Jubal wanted to kill him fast.

The shot was difficult. Jubal was stretched out on the floor, angling the Colt at Klein's head, anxious to avoid hitting the boy. It would have struck clean, blowing the albino's face away, if Andy hadn't thrown himself back at that precise instant. The boy was trying to give Jubal a clear field of fire;

140

instead, he dragged Klein down so that the bullet went past his snarling face. Klein swore and hit Andy hard along the side of his jaw. The blow smashed the youngster backwards, knocking him flat. As he fell, the gunman triggered the S&W, his shot creasing a streamer of blood across Jubal's cheek.

Jubal thumbed back the Colt's hammer, aiming for Klein's chest. There was a sharp *click*, but no detonation. Klein laughed and fired again. Jubal was rolling sideways and the shot missed him, blowing splinters from the floor. Furiously, he worked the hammer, spinning the cylinder of the Peacemaker. Again, the handgun failed to fire. He cursed and threw the jammed weapon at Klein's head. The albino ducked and Jubal ran for the stairs. The forgotten saloon was built on two levels, the narrow staircase reaching up to a balcony that ran around the walls. In several places, the woodwork was rotted through, and the stairs groaned ominously as Jubal raced up them. He got to the balcony and kicked a dusty chair down the stairs. Klein hung back, watching the planking above.

'Where you figger to go?' He stared up. 'You're cornered.'

He punctuated the sentence with a bullet.

Jubal hugged the wall as the .44 shell lifted a cloud of dust a foot away from his toes. There was a second shot, and he saw a plank jerk upwards as the bullet tore it loose. He moved fast, running to the rear of the building. Klein chuckled and spaced three shots along the balcony. Jubal heard the explosions and felt something tear at his heel. He risked looking back and saw Andy Prescott moving cautiously along the perimeter of the saloon, heading for the door. He hoped the boy would get away safe.

Klein was standing at the foot of the stairs, watching for Jubal to show. He dropped the empty gun into the holster and drew the matching pistol. Jubal grasped a chair and tossed it across the balcony. Klein fired twice as it hit, bouncing the chair back up in the air. When the thunder died away, Jubal was crouched in the angle of the rear and side walls, wondering about his chances of staying alive. Klein spaced three more bullets through the balcony floor and began to reload.

141

Working with professional speed, he snapped the break-open chamber, spent cartridge cases ejecting to the side. He held the gun in his left hand as he pulled fresh shells from his coat pocket and dropped them into the magazine. Then he cocked the Russian and set it down by his right foot. Deft and fast, he repeated the performance with the other gun. Then he stood up, a revolver in both hands, and began to climb the stairs.

He was halfway up when Jubal saw Andy. The boy was carrying the Spencer, heading for the centre of the saloon as though he could see where he was going.

'Jubal?' His voice betrayed his fear. 'Where are you, Jubal?'

'Here!'

Jubal's answer ripped from between tight-clenched lips as he powered forwards and up from the angle of the walls. He hit the balcony rail with both hands and lifted over. The balcony was fifteen feet off the floor and when he hit it felt like his legs had been driven up through his ribs. He landed on both feet, rolling as Klein appeared at the head of the stairs.

'Here, Andy!'

He ignored the pain in his side, rage-induced adrenalin pumping energy through his tensed body. Andy heard him and ran forwards, holding out the Spencer. Jubal grabbed the rifle and shoved Andy roughly away as he powered to the side. The boy staggered, almost losing his footing, and stood, staring blindly around the empty room.

Klein showed above the balcony. He had the S&W Russians in both hands. Flame blazed from the muzzles. Jubal levered the Spencer, squeezing down on the trigger as the mechanism pumped a shell into the breech. The hammer lifted back and fell. He pumped the action again.

Klein was emptying both the handguns in Jubal's direction, and splinters blasted from the floor around the smaller man. Jubal felt a bullet tear through his suit, another rip the bandage over his ribs. There was a sudden flash of pain in his left arm, but he ignored it as he pumped the Spencer's action, firing faster than he had ever done.

He saw the bullets plough heavy chunks of wood from the balcony rail. And snarled like a cornered wolf. And kept on firing.

Saul Klein jerked suddenly, a shocked expression appearing on his death-white face. He stared down, his mouth opening, and dropped one of the Russians. Then his mouth snapped shut as a bullet tore through the back of his neck. His left hand reached over to touch the hole in his stomach. And closed tight over the material of his vest as a bright red hole flowered in the centre of his forehead. It was redder than his eyes, and a heavy droplet of crimson welled out, trickling sluggishly over his nose. He opened his mouth again, but when he did only blood came out, and his shout was thick and unintelligible. He fired the remaining S&W into the floor. Then he doubled over, falling heavily against the balcony rail. The rotted wood gave way and he crashed through, pitching to the floor below. A great cloud of dust lifted up as he hit, then settled over his black-clad corpse. It mingled with the blood pumping from his face and stomach and chest, thickening the flow so that it slowed, surging dustily over his body as though tired by the effort. His red eyes stared up at the ceiling, sightless now, and a deep exhalation raised dust from his bloody lips. Then he was still.

Jubal turned, the Spencer clutched in both hands. His knuckles shone white where he gripped the rifle, but the tension was going from his face, the mask of hate and rage easing off.

He turned to Andy. The boy was standing close by the stairs, smiling.

'You got him, Jubal?'

'Sure, son,' he answered. 'It took a while, but you settled it with the rifle. Now we can go home.'

'Paw had a saying for it,' murmured the boy. His voice sounded slightly breathless. 'A friend in need is a friend in deed.'

'You sure were,' said Jubal, grinning.

'So were you,' replied Andy. 'The best friend I ever had.'

Then he fell forwards. He fell like a puppet with its strings cut, his knees suddenly bending so that he simply pitched face-down onto the dirty floor. Jubal cried out and came across the room in three long strides. When he reached Andy, he could see the blood coming out of the hole in the boy's back. It was a big hole, and the ragged edges of his shirt were already thick with blood. When he turned him over he saw the small, neat hole in his chest. It was very small. It didn't look big enough to kill anyone, and there was hardly any blood around it.

But Andy's face was desperately pale, pinched in so that he looked very young. And very dead. Jubal lifted him, staring into open blue eyes that would never, now, learn to see again.

And he screamed. It came up from the pit of his belly, ripping through his lungs and bursting from his drawn-back lips like the lonesome wailing of a lobo wolf. It went on and on as the tears filled his eyes and ran down his cheeks, and great shudders racked his bent-over body. It contained rage, and hate. But mostly it contained loss, a grief too deep to put into words; a lament for life and hope and dreams that went on keening, building echoes off the walls of the deserted, lonely saloon until the place rang with his cries.

He lowered Andy's body gently onto the floor and went out to his horse. He left the emptied Spencer where it lay as he dragged the medical valise from the bay pony's saddle. He began to fumble his instruments out as he went back into the saloon.

But he knew they would do no good.